BATTLING C   !

Andrew, being bigger and older than Felix, and having a far better grip, wrenched the basket from Felix's hands and heaved it over the rail. Over and over it tumbled in the air before splashing into the murky water below. Felix started turning purple with sheer rage.

"What did you do that for? You stuck-up little Hetty's pet!"

Vengefully, Felix flew at Andrew, trying to grab a great handful of his cousin's hair. Taken by surprise, Andrew lost his footing as he tried to fend off his attacker. As he fell, Andrew took Felix with him. The next moment the two boys were rolling about on the bridge pummeling each other for all they were worth. Sara jumped out of range barely in time to avoid being knocked down herself.

"Felix! Andrew!" she cried frantically. "Someone's gonna get hurt!"

But hurting someone was just what both boys were bent on. Seeing that she could do nothing herself, Sara turned around and dashed away to get help.

**Also available in the Road to Avonlea series
from Bantam Skylark books**

Family Rivalry

Storybook written by

Gail Hamilton

Based on the Sullivan Films Production
written by Jerome McCann
adapted from the novels of

Lucy Maud Montgomery

A BANTAM SKYLARK BOOK®
NEW YORK · TORONTO · LONDON · SYDNEY · AUCKLAND

Based on the Sullivan Films Production produced by Sullivan Films Inc.
in association with CBC and the Disney Channel with the participation
of Telefilm Canada adapted from Lucy Maud Montgomery's novels.

Teleplay written by Jerome McCann.
Copyright © 1991 by Sullivan Films Distribution, Inc.

This edition contains the complete text
of the original edition.
NOT ONE WORD HAS BEEN OMITTED.

RL 6, 008–012

FAMILY RIVALRY
A Bantam Skylark Book / published by arrangement with
HarperCollins Publishers Ltd.

PUBLISHING HISTORY
HarperCollins edition published 1992
Bantam edition / July 1993

ROAD TO AVONLEA is the trademark of Sullivan Films Inc.

Skylark Books is a registered trademark of Bantam Books,
a division of Bantam Doubleday Dell Publishing Group, Inc.
Registered in U.S. Patent and Trademark Office and elsewhere.

All rights reserved.
Storybook written by Gail Hamilton.
Copyright © 1992 by HarperCollins Publishers, Sullivan Films
Distribution, Inc., and Ruth Macdonald and David Macdonald.
No part of this book may be reproduced or transmitted in any form or by any means,
electronic or mechanical, including photocopying, recording, or by any information
storage and retrieval system, without permission in writing from the publisher.
For information address: HarperCollins Publishers Ltd., Suite 2900,
Hazelton Lanes, 55 Avenue Road, Toronto, Canada M5R 3L2.

ISBN 0-553-48042-1

Bantam Books are published by Bantam Books, a division of Bantam Doubleday Dell
Publishing Group, Inc. Its trademark, consisting of the words "Bantam Books" and the
portrayal of a rooster, is Registered in U.S. Patent and Trademark Office and in other
countries. Marca Registrada. Bantam Books, 1540 Broadway, New York, New York 10036.

PRINTED IN THE UNITED STATES OF AMERICA
OPM   0 9 8 7 6 5 4 3 2 1

Chapter One

A high-wheeled buggy rattled merrily towards the King farm, carrying Alec, Janet and Felix King. All of them basked in the sun-drenched day. With gulls wheeling overhead and a tangy breeze blowing in off the sea, the weather seemed made-to-order for bolstering good humor; it had been a fine day for paying a social call.

"Hard to believe," Alec mused, steering the horse skillfully around a pothole, "how Malcolm and Abigail's little boy has grown."

Abigail, Janet King's sister, had waited long to marry and even longer for motherhood.

Motherhood had come to Abigail in the form of an adorable orphan literally left on her doorstep. The child was a thriving toddler now, filling Abigail and her husband with so much delight that the whole community had to smile every time the pair walked their pride-and-joy down the street.

Alec's mind was on children as, beside him, Janet was growing large with the promise of yet another King youngster. The baby was awaited with mounting anticipation by everyone—and with more than a little anxiety by Felix.

"I don't want another sister, Mother," Felix insisted from the back seat. He already had two sisters—one older, who bossed him around, and one younger, who was far more interested in her best friend, Clemmie Ray, than in him. The closest thing he had to a brother, at the moment, was his cousin Andrew, who was staying at the farm while his father finished important work in South America.

"Well, Dr. Blair said there's a possibility of twins," Janet murmured complacently.

Felix was filled with galloping alarm! One new sister would be bad enough—but two! Surely that was more girls than any fellow could be asked to put up with in one lifetime!

"One brother would be enough for me," he informed his mother hurriedly, hoping to impress her with the modesty of his demands.

"Well, having a brother isn't always easy. Your father and Uncle Roger certainly had their share of disagreements, didn't you, Alec?"

Janet King smiled mischievously towards her husband, an easy-going, sunburnt farmer edging towards middle age.

Alec hesitated as he struggled with some uncomfortable memories. "Well, we had our disappointments over the years," he admitted, "but I wouldn't say we didn't get along."

He only succeeded in making his wife laugh. Janet had grown up in Avonlea, too, and had known Alec King for about as long as she could remember—certainly long before she had had any thoughts of marrying him. It was impossible for Alec to hide anything from her.

"Oh Alec, you and Roger never saw eye to eye on anything."

"Is Uncle Roger as famous as Aunt Hetty says he is?" Felix wanted to know. "She makes him sound smarter than a professor and more important than the Prime Minister!" His Aunt Hetty, who was even older than his father, and who had never married anybody, was apt to get pretty windy about anything she considered important. Years of teaching school did that to a person, Felix supposed. He himself had had to listen to enough of Aunt Hetty's high-flown speeches at the Avonlea school.

Janet paused, choosing her words carefully. Hetty was the eldest of the Kings and considered herself the head of the clan—an idea that had already caused enough head-butting in the family to last Janet a lifetime. Janet didn't want to stir up the waters now any more than necessary.

"Well...um...your Aunt Hetty always did favor your Uncle Roger, Felix."

This was one of those statements loaded with a whole world of meaning, most of it too complicated for Felix to figure out at the moment.

"I must say, he's done well for himself, considering," Alec added quickly, as though in a hurry to give Roger his full due.

"Oh, well!" Janet clasped her hands in admiration of her brother-in-law. "He's one of the most sought-after geologists in the country."

Felix had certainly heard enough about the geology part from his cousin Andrew, who was Roger's son. The minute Andrew had heard his father was on his way back from Brazil, he had started spending most of his time digging in the fields and poking along the riverbank so he could make a rock collection of his own.

"I can't wait to meet him again." Felix's own memories of his uncle were very dim, but it was exciting to have a real celebrity in the family.

As the buggy rolled up to the rambling King farmhouse, Janet grinned at her husband.

"Remember," she chuckled, "when Roger pushed you out of the barn door into the manure pile? You went face first out on the—"

"Janet!" Alec exclaimed mildly. He didn't want the old incident raked up again for the amusement of his son. Some boyhood things remain sensitive, even to a grown man. Alec pointed to a buggy tied to the yard fence—a quick and handy way to change the subject.

"Now, looks like Dr. Blair has been here waiting a while. Whoa!"

He reined in the horse and pulled to a halt. Felix hopped down and held out his hands to help his mother as she clambered to the ground. Alec remained in his seat.

"And...uh...well, I've got some things to pick up at Lawson's," Alec told his wife, and he clucked the horse into a trot again before any more tales of his childhood could surface to plague him.

As Alec drove off, Janet took a firm grip of her son's hand and started towards the house, where the doctor waited to give her a checkup.

"Please finish the story, Mother," Felix demanded, trotting to keep up. He didn't intend to be done out of a story in which his father had ended up in a manure heap!

"Well," began his mother happily, "it all started when Roger and your father were raising pigs for the Charlottetown fair. They couldn't decide which one of them should parade the pigs in front of the judge, so..."

Alec was gratefully out of earshot as Janet told the embarrassing story. He drove past the barn, his lips pressed rather tightly together, and gave the horse a slap with the reins. In no time at all, he was rumbling over the covered bridge and into the nearby village of Avonlea.

Alec tied his horse up in front of the general store, the heart of this rural village. The store was a comfortable wooden building with a long veranda and heaps of goods visible through the wide-paned windows. Mr. and Mrs. Lawson ran this establishment, and, between them, they managed to cope with just about every commercial need the people in the neighborhood could come up with.

Alec walked in to see Mrs. Lawson behind the counter serving a worried-looking man with his arm in a sling. The man was Amos Spry, one of the local farmers. His worn clothes, callused hands and diffident air attested to a life not always on the best of terms with good luck and prosperity.

"Hello, Alec," Mrs. Lawson called out pleasantly as she made up parcels for her customer. She wore a large apron over her dress and was perfectly at home among the stacks of items rising up to the ceiling around her.

"Hello," Amos echoed, managing to wipe the anxious expression off his face long enough to greet Alec.

Alec nodded back, prepared to wait his turn. He had to step round a man and a woman who were standing by the front door. The woman was holding a shirt up against the man's chest in an effort to check the size. Getting any man to actually try on a shirt inside the general store was a hopeless expectation.

Just as Alec was making himself comfortable, he was startled by the shrieks of two young children who suddenly tore past. A boy of about seven chased an even younger girl, playing tag with complete abandon among the heaped goods and the legs of the customers. The dark hair, skinny bodies and pointed chins marked them clearly as two of Amos's offspring. Mrs. Spry had babies so regularly that people in Avonlea had lost count. Every year Amos looked more harried, and a new Spry appeared at the school to give Hetty King another gray hair or two.

Perhaps Amos was so used to being awash in children that he didn't pay attention to them any more. Right then, certainly, Amos seemed to be watching the additions to his bill so closely that he was oblivious to the antics of his young ones. Mrs. Lawson, in the interests of smooth commerce, politely pretended that the children's behavior didn't bother her, even though they represented a fearful danger to her jars of pickling spices and the row of fancy glass lamp globes on shelves quite within their reach.

"I got you cornered!" the boy crowed, leaping to tag his sister in a spot just under Mrs. Lawson's display of cups and saucers. Young Stephen was so quick on his feet that his sister, May, didn't have a hope of escape.

Mrs. Lawson put a bag of flour on the counter next to Amos's other purchases, which seemed scanty for such a large family.

"I don't know where they get their energy," she said, eyeing the children and trying not to grimace. "I really don't."

Making sure to keep out of the way, Alec started browsing casually among the hats. Even there, he wasn't safe, for little May ran smack into his knee.

"Children, that's enough, now," he told them, catching the wrinkle in Mrs. Lawson's brow.

They were good children, even though rambunctious. At the reprimand from Alec, they stopped their wild racing and stood, at least temporarily, still. The gaze of both then went straight to the tempting array of peppermint sticks in a big glass jar by the cash register. Stephen trotted over to his father and tugged at his sleeve.

"Can we have a candy stick, Papa?"

Amos frowned and bent over, trying to speak quietly so as not to be overheard by the entire store.

"Maybe some other time, son. Don't want to spoil your appetite."

"Spoil our appetite?" Stephen cried, entirely defeating his father's efforts at discretion. "We just ate!"

Mrs. Lawson quietly totted up the bill, hoping

to get the children through the door and out of her store as soon as possible.

"That'll be two dollars and ten cents."

Instead of reaching for his pocketbook, Amos shifted on his feet, looked furtively around him and then leaned towards Mrs. Lawson.

"Could you see your way to putting that on my account?" he asked, in the lowest of confidential tones.

"Oh, Amos..." Mrs. Lawson looked distressed in a way that did not bode well for Amos's request.

Alec looked up from the hat display, unable to help overhearing what was going on.

"I'm afraid I've already overextended your credit," Mrs. Lawson said uncomfortably. "Now, I told you last time..."

Looking over at her father, May reached up and caressed a doll on display. The doll was a pretty one, with curly yellow hair and a painted china smile. Passionate longing gleamed in May's eyes, making it clear that the little Sprys did not have a lot in the way of toys.

"I know, I know," Amos pleaded, glancing regretfully at his daughter and the doll, "but if you could just give me a couple of weeks till I get the harvest in, I'd be able to settle with you then."

May, unaware of her father's troubles, ran her fingers softly along the flounces of the doll's dress. Oh, a doll like that simply begged to be cradled in a little girl's arms—and that was what May wanted to do more than anything. Giving in to the temptation, she stood on tiptoe to reach up and bring the doll down. Unfortunately, May's small hands knocked a can of custard powder over from the shelf behind. Naturally, the can tumbled straight into a box of fresh eggs, breaking a good many of the ones on top.

Mrs. Lawson gasped in dismay, and Amos groaned, as though he just couldn't believe his ongoing misfortunes.

"Oh, May, what have you done?" he lamented, straightening up from the counter.

Silence fell inside the store. Young May, caught hugging the doll and standing over the egg box, felt all eyes upon her. She clutched the doll even closer and immediately burst into tears. She knew she had broken the eggs and eggs cost money and there wasn't any money at all in her daddy's pockets.

Alec, being nearest, quickly reached over and removed the child from the mess.

"There, there," he told her soothingly, patting her on the back and putting the doll safely back on its shelf. "You'll be all right."

May didn't believe this for one minute. She only wailed the louder, scrubbing at her eyes with her fists. Mrs. Lawson, really a kindhearted person and herself flustered by all the crying, rushed to smooth out the situation. She also knew that if Amos couldn't pay for his current purchases, he certainly wasn't going to be able to make good on the eggs. The eggs, at least, would have to be written off.

"Now, it's all right, Amos," she told him. "Accidents happen."

With his arm already in a sling, Amos knew that for sure.

"Calm down, now," Alec said to the wailing May, trying to coax her out of her fright.

Fat tears were rolling down May's face and plopping onto her carefully mended dress. Not only that, Stephen's lips were quivering, too, as he threatened to join May in vigorous duet.

"Why don't you take the children home," Mrs. Lawson said to Amos, defeated by the situation and only wanting the Sprys safely out of the store, "and...uh, I'll put it on your account."

With a sigh of relief, which he tried mightily to hide, Amos tipped his cap.

"Thanks, Elvira. I'm...I'm real sorry."

Chapter Two

Outside the store, Amos wanted nothing more than to escape, but it wasn't easy with only one good arm. Stephen and May each carried a small parcel, and Amos struggled with his big wicker basket, trying to figure out how to get the rest of his purchases up onto his wagon.

Back in the store, Alec paused and took two peppermint sticks from the jar young Stephen had been eyeing.

"Maybe I'll take a couple of these, Elvira," he said to the storekeeper, handing her a coin.

Mrs. Lawson knew perfectly well who the candy was for. She slipped the coin into the cash drawer, hoping that the money wasn't the only profit she was going to see that day in her transactions with the Sprys.

Alec picked up Amos's bag of flour from the counter and stepped outside where he found the Spry children sitting hunched on the store steps, May still sobbing loudly and Stephen looking almost as woebegone. Alec stooped down and produced the candy sticks.

"Here. You think you can use one of these?"

Two sets of eyes popped wide at the bounty.

"Thanks," Stephen remembered to say just before he stuck the candy into his mouth.

The peppermint had an equally magical effect upon May, whose tears dried instantly.

"Thank you," she murmured, a small smile appearing among the tear smudges on her face.

Amos, with difficulty, was shoving the basket over the tailgate of his wagon when Alec joined him. Alec plunked the bag of flour in beside the basket and leaned on the side of the vehicle.

"Thanks, Alec," Amos offered.

"One of those days, is it, Amos?" Alec asked sympathetically.

Amos sighed heavily. "Every day's been one of those days lately, Alec," he muttered, wincing as his sling bumped one of the wheels.

"Come on," Alec cajoled, "it can't be as bad as that."

Since Amos didn't look up and his face grew tighter, Alec realized something serious must be going on.

"What's the problem?" he inquired gently, for troubles were generally shared among neighbors.

"Money and luck, neither of which seems to come my way these days. I'm in a bad spot of trouble, Alec." Amos grimaced, and, after a pause, he added in a rush, "I stand to lose the farm."

Alec's hand, halfway to pushing back his hat, stopped in midair.

"Go on—you're not serious!"

Apparently, he was, for Amos heaved a sigh, pointing to his sling.

"My horse ran off, I fell and broke my arm, missed a couple of payments in the past three months. Bank says I'm a bad risk. They've decided not to extend my loan."

"But that's nonsense," Alec protested. "Everyone knows there's gonna be a bumper potato crop this year."

Potatoes were what nearly everyone grew on Prince Edward Island. The province was famous for them. Why, right at that very moment, Alec thought, markets everywhere were waiting for the new crop to come in!

Pessimistically, Amos shook his head. Fate seemed to have a special grudge against him.

"Well, maybe for everyone else. For me, it'll only be fair, at best."

"There's no reason why you shouldn't have an excellent crop, Amos," Alec asserted firmly in the face of Amos's gloom.

Though he knew Alec was right, Amos only looked more despondent. With his arm in a sling, he couldn't do much about even the best crop in the world. Things were very bad indeed.

"All I need's a few more weeks. If I could just get my crop in and be able to start paying off my mortgage again..."

A neighbor in trouble was a man to be helped, at least in Alec's book. If farmers didn't look out for each other, no one else was going to.

"I can help you get your crop in," Alec offered.

"I appreciate that, Alec," Amos said, with feeling, "but it still won't solve my problem."

Only money was going to solve the problem, and Alec saw that clearly. He sucked in a breath, not deterred by the size of the risk he was about to take.

"Well, how about if...I go along to the bank and co-sign for the loan?"

This was an offer well beyond the call of neighborliness. Amos looked up in wonder.

"I don't understand," he said shakily.

Leaning on the wagon wheel, Alec calculated rapidly. The children, still blissfully sucking their candy sticks, strolled over, ready to go home.

"If I co-signed the mortgage, then...well...in the unlikely event that your crop doesn't come through, the bank will still get their money." Of course, the money the bank would get would be Alec King's and not Amos Spry's.

Easily, Alec lifted Stephen up onto the wagon seat. Amos swallowed hard and looked at his benefactor.

"You'd do that for me, Alec?"

Amos knew a lot of folks in Avonlea looked down on the Sprys, what with all their children and their continual struggle to make ends meet. Yet here was Alec King, just about the most respected farmer around, offering to put up his own money to guarantee Amos's loan.

Alec deposited May on the seat beside her brother and nodded. "Of course. That's what neighbors are for, Amos."

With that, Alec walked back to the store leaving Amos speechless from sheer relief and gratitude. The horrible vision of Mrs. Spry and all the little Sprys homeless by the side of the road left Amos's imagination. Looking as though a thousand-pound weight had just been lifted from his shoulders, the man climbed up beside his children and pointed the horse for home.

Chapter Three

Growing up on a farm meant that Felix always had plenty of chores to do and had learned to work hard. He wasn't always happy about being stuck with so much work. He would much rather be down by the river, fishing for trout. Haying season had arrived, however, and there was no respite for Felix.

Not long after Alec co-signed for Amos Spry's loan, Felix and Andrew found themselves in a field near the house pitching hay and hoeing potatoes. Andrew was older than Felix, close to fourteen, a slender, thoughtful boy. He suddenly broke off hoeing to pick up a stone.

"Aren't you finished yet?" Felix demanded, slinging another forkful of hay.

Felix was a sturdy, straightforward fellow who sometimes lost patience with his more introspective cousin. Andrew, he felt, had been pampered far too much before coming to the King farm. He was sure he could have hoed those potatoes himself in half the time.

Leaning on his hoe, Andrew held the rock up to the sun to see the light glinting off its glassy sides.

"A piece of quartz," he explained to Felix,

who had absolutely no interest in rocks, quartz or otherwise. "Don't usually find a rock like that on P.E.I."

Carefully, Andrew placed his prize in an old wicker fishing basket standing by his side. Felix caught sight of the basket and all but dropped his pitchfork when he suddenly recognized it.

"That's Grandpa King's fishing basket, isn't it?"

Andrew nodded, turning his attention back to the potatoes. "Aunt Hetty gave it to me as a going-away present when she heard that my father was coming back to get me."

How dare Aunt Hetty just hand out family property to whoever took her fancy! A thundercloud darkened Felix's face.

"But it was promised to *me*," he burst out indignantly. "And besides, you don't even fish."

Felix had had his heart set on that basket ever since he could remember. He had been allowed to carry it when he was just a little fellow, trotting at Grandpa King's side on their way to the fishing hole. Grandpa King had taught Felix to fish, and the basket remind him of all the happy times spent with his grandfather. More than that, Felix also regarded it as lucky. On the day when he could finally use it for his own fishing tackle, he was sure his catch would double, or even triple! And now his Aunt Hetty had just casually given it away to a boy who spent his spare time reading and didn't know one end of a fishing pole from the other.

"I use it to store my rock collection," Andrew replied complacently, not seeing how upset Felix had become.

Felix grew still angrier. Andrew didn't even know how to take care of the basket!

"You can't put rocks in there. You'll ruin it!"

The argument was broken off by the arrival of Sara Stanley and Felicity King carrying a basket full of sandwiches and a pitcher of cold water.

"Lunch is here, Felix. Come and eat," called Sara, setting the pitcher down on the grass.

There was nothing Felix loved better than to eat, and ordinarily the prospect of lunch would have cheered him immensely. Today, fuming over the fishing basket, he jammed his pitchfork into the earth and walked, in a less than cordial mood, over to the two girls.

"It's about time," he grumbled sulkily.

Sara pulled back the napkin over the food and called towards the potato patch.

"Andrew, Aunt Hetty wants to see you."

Gladly, Andrew put down his hoe and joined the others. He accepted a huge chicken sandwich on homemade bread. Sara watched him take an appreciative bite.

"When is your father supposed to arrive?" she asked, knowing the big event had to be sometime pretty soon.

Though he would never have said so, Andrew had missed his father terribly. The months spent with the King family had been happy ones, but aunts and uncles couldn't substitute for a fellow's father. He looked up with a glowing face.

"In about a week, if all goes well. I've been adding quite a bit to my rock collection. I hope he's impressed with it."

"I'm sure he will be," Sara assured him, smiling. Hadn't they all helped him hunt for specimens, ever since he began his busy search? Sara was a perceptive girl, and she saw how important it was to Andrew to make an impression upon the famous man who had been absent from his life for so long.

"Well, I'm gonna go see what Aunt Hetty wants," Andrew said, starting towards Rose Cottage.

Truth to tell, Andrew was glad to get away

from the hoe and the potatoes, so he set out while still eating his sandwich. Luckily, Rose Cottage was just a hop and a skip away from the rambling King farmhouse.

As Andrew left, though, he didn't forget to take his fishing basket with him. Felix glowered after him, seeing how heavily the basket weighed on Andrew's arm. It must be chock full of rocks, he thought. It could fall apart any minute from the strain!

"Aunt Hetty?" Andrew called as he reached Rose Cottage and toiled with his heavy load up the porch steps.

Rose Cottage was a pretty, gabled house with a white picket fence and wide verandas all around. Inside, Hetty was sitting in the parlor reading. At the sound of Andrew's voice, she whipped off her glasses and smiled in anticipation.

She was an angular, middle-aged woman of prim appearance and formidable posture. With her hair swept up into a huge bun and a watch always pinned at her breast, she could intimidate both in the classroom and out, and could argue a fixed opinion with the tenacity of half a dozen bulldogs. Particular as she was about the prestige of the King clan and the status of herself as a leader of the community, many people found Hetty a prickly woman to deal with. She softened all over, though, at the sight of her nephew.

"Andrew, there you are." She greeted him warmly as he came into the parlor, still lugging the basket.

"Sara said you wanted to see me."

With an air of delicious mystery, Hetty picked up an envelope that had been lying beside her on the couch. Her eyes twinkled as she held it out.

"Indeed I do. I picked this up at the post office this morning. It's for you."

"What is it?" Andrew asked, baffled by such an unexpected turn of events.

Hetty's smile grew even wider; she could barely hide her own excitement.

"Open it and find out!"

Andrew tore open the envelope and extracted a crisp, official-looking sheet.

"It's from the Superintendent of Education," he murmured in puzzlement.

Unable to contain herself any longer, Hetty snatched the letter from her nephew.

"A special citation is what it is, for your science essay." Hetty was almost bursting with pride.

"Almost forgotten about that," Andrew said modestly, a little uncomfortable in the face of Hetty's excitement.

"Oh, your father's going to be supremely proud of you!" Hetty beamed, as pleased as though she had received the citation herself. She paused and gestured towards her desk. "Come over here, Andrew. Sit down."

Careful of his overalls, Andrew sat down in the polished chair. Hetty reached past him into the drawer and took out a great bundle of papers tied up with a blue ribbon. Many were yellowed at the edges and dog-eared from handling. Hetty held the lot to her bosom for a moment before she set it down on the desk before Andrew.

"I haven't shown you this before," Hetty confided, "but I think now is the time. It is a collection of each and every one of your father's report cards and science tests. There are also a few published articles he's sent me over the years."

Hetty seemed to be actually expanding with pride now, and Andrew lit up at the sight of the mementoes. He worshiped his father and thought anything connected with him utterly wonderful.

"Really? I'd like to read these, if I could."

"It would be time well spent, don't you think?" Hetty agreed, with complete disregard for all the rows of potatoes still waiting to be hoed.

Chapter Four

While Andrew was spending his time pleasantly in the comfort of the Rose Cottage parlor, Felix was seething with dissatisfaction. The minute the last of the sandwiches from the lunch basket had been gulped down, he went straight to his father with his grievance. He didn't even wait to finish loading the hay wagon. He found Alec down by the river—the very same river in which all the generations of Kings had fished. As they walked along the bank, Felix pitched pebbles angrily into the water.

"You know I always loved that fishing basket," he was saying furiously as Alec followed along behind.

"Mm-hmm," was all Alec answered, staying noncommittal until he had heard all the facts of the matter. As a father of three, he had had a lot of experience sorting out children's squabbles.

"And Grandpa King promised it to me," Felix

added, delivering what he considered to be the clinching argument. "Now Andrew's got it full of dumb rocks!"

It certainly was true that a fishing basket didn't seem the right place to keep rocks. Alec patted his son reassuringly on the shoulder.

"Well, settle down, Felix. Maybe there's been a misunderstanding. But don't forget, Grandpa King was Andrew's grandfather, too."

Alec well remembered how much a boy could love a fishing basket—especially the very basket Andrew was toting about with him. That basket, after all, had belonged to Alec's father. As a young lad, Alec had fished from it, too, and he wanted Felix to be able to enjoy it the same way.

Felix, only partly mollified, could only think of the heavy, sharp-edged rock collection.

"It's already half ruined," he complained grumpily.

"Well, it'll all be settled once I talk to your Aunt Hetty," Alec assured him. He wished Hetty wouldn't make these impulsive moves without consulting all the people concerned.

Back at Rose Cottage, Hetty had drawn up a chair beside Andrew at the desk. The two of them were happily poring over Roger King's old report cards and carefully handwritten essays. Andrew touched them reverently, as though they would somehow bring him nearer to his father.

"He got straight As," the boy breathed, with something like awe.

Pride again illuminated Hetty's countenance. As a schoolteacher, she could well appreciate every aspect of Roger's achievements. Academic glory was very important to her.

"Oh, and due entirely to Roger's own hard work and discipline. Though I will confess," Hetty chuckled, "the As in English Literature were due in large part to my tutoring."

Andrew peered round at his aunt, who so obviously loved learning and was so pleased with what she had been able to do for his father. A sudden thought struck him.

"Why didn't you go to university, Aunt Hetty?"

The question quite startled Hetty out of her reverie. She remained silent for a moment over the yellowing essays and couldn't help looking suddenly regretful.

"In those days, well, it was acceptable for an intelligent woman to...become a teacher. Yes, but...but the idea of higher education...no, no, no. Simply not possible."

Hetty had to leave unsaid just what prodigies she might have accomplished had she ever had a chance at a degree, because Andrew had spotted Alec and Felix coming up the front walk. Guiltily, he remembered his farm duties. He swept his father's report cards into a neat pile and started to get up.

"Excuse me, Aunt Hetty, but I have to milk the cows, so..."

Instantly, Hetty had her hand on his shoulder, easing him back down into his chair. She gave a negligent wave in Alec's direction.

"Pish-posh. You've only a short while left in Avonlea. No, your time's better spent with me. Get one of the others to do the chores for you."

As Felix and Alec trooped into the house, Andrew looked dubious about Hetty's order. Uncle Alec was a stickler about everyone pulling their weight.

"Hetty!" Alec called out, shutting the door behind him.

"Alec?" Hetty called out, as though she didn't already know who was in the hall.

Alec and Felix stepped through the French doors into the parlor, bent on business. Hetty, who saw only an extra pair of useful young hands, twisted round in her chair.

"Ah, Felix...how fortunate. I was just thinking of you. I want you to do the milking for Andrew this afternoon. He'll be very busy, you see.".

"He's what?" Felix exclaimed incredulously. All he could see was Andrew lounging about in front of a lot of old papers with nothing, apparently, to do but twiddle his thumbs.

"Busy," Hetty repeated.

Then, seeing the incomprehension on Felix's face, Hetty couldn't resist being a bit harsh. Unlike Andrew, who had shone all year in class, Felix seemed to have little inclination for book learning. And he certainly couldn't have imagined spending a sunny afternoon poring over old school reports.

"Not that difficult to understand, Felix," Hetty told the boy, emphasizing each word as though for a slower intellect, *I want you to milk the cows.*"

Alec drew his brows together in irritation. Sometimes Hetty went too far. And when it came to interfering with farm work, Alec was going to have none of it.

"Hetty, I need to have a word with you," he said firmly. Then he turned to Andrew and Felix.

"Now, you boys can run along. Andrew, I do want you to milk the cows, despite what your Aunt Hetty says."

With a rueful glance at his aunt, Andrew got up and followed Felix out onto the front steps. He didn't forget to take the fishing basket, either, which made Felix even more irate.

"That's *my* fishing basket," Felix shouted at Andrew as he reached the front gate and jerked it open.

Since all he got was a glower from Andrew, Felix dashed off, leaving the matter to his father to straighten out.

Andrew followed slowly, holding the basket protectively to him. The basket was his because his Aunt Hetty had said so, and that was that! Oh, he hoped so very much that his father was going to be impressed with his collection.

Back in the parlor, Alec stepped across the rug and leaned over Hetty, more than a little annoyed.

"Hetty, what the devil are you doing, getting Felix to do Andrew's chores?"

Busying herself with tying up Roger's papers again, Hetty merely glanced at her brother.

"Really, Alec, the boy has far too much potential

to waste his time doing chores. Besides, I've given him some important reading to do."

Small muscles started to play along Alec's jaw. It was almost as though the words were coming back to him from his own long-ago childhood.

"Chores teach a boy responsibility."

Chin lifted patronizingly, Hetty put on her best schoolmistress look.

"A boy of Andrew's calibre needs to exercise his mind far more than his muscles. It appears that he has, fortunately, inherited Roger's intellect."

Something about the way Hetty said "Roger's intellect" caused Alec's face to stiffen even more.

"Ah, so you're trying to turn him into a bookworm," he said sharply. "Look, all the boy needs is a normal upbringing. And besides," Alec leaped straight to his son's grievance, "you had absolutely no business giving him Father's fishing basket."

"I see no point in getting riled over a decrepit old basket."

"A decrepit old—!" Alec stopped short rather than lose his temper. "You wouldn't even let Felix touch the thing."

"Oh, really, Alec," Hetty sputtered, trying to wave him away.

"Besides," Alec barreled on, refusing to be diverted, "you know Father promised that basket to Felix for his twelfth birthday."

That birthday was only a few months away. No wonder Felix had been so upset! Yet, as if the matter were of no importance, Hetty merely shrugged.

"Good grief! You don't expect me to take it back now, do you?"

Alec most certainly did. And he was just about to say so when Olivia, the youngest of Alec's sisters, suddenly rushed into the room, so agog with excitement she could barely get out her news.

"Hetty...Alec...it's Roger," she gasped. "He's here!"

Chapter Five

Andrew hadn't been in Rose Cottage to hear the news of his father's early arrival. Consequently, he was walking slowly towards the King farmhouse, quite oblivious to the man driving the horse and buggy in the same direction. Wrapped up in his own thoughts, he paid no attention until the horse came to a halt beside the front door of the farmhouse, shook its bridle and neighed, making Andrew lift his head.

For a long moment, Andrew's eyes blinked in sheer disbelief. Then his face was transformed by pure joy.

"Father!" he shouted, and he started running as fast as his legs would carry him towards the buggy.

Roger King, who had just climbed down in front of the gate, turned to the racing boy.

"Andrew!"

"Father, you're here!" Andrew cannonballed into the man's arms and gave him a terrific hug. "I missed you, Papa."

"And I missed you, too," Roger said hoarsely, hugging the boy tightly again.

A moment later, Roger released Andrew, took him by the shoulders and stood back a little.

"Well, let me look at you," he murmured, scanning the boy fondly from top to toe. "My God, how you've grown."

A year was a very long time for a father to be away from a son just verging on fourteen. Fourteen was a tumultuous time of life, full of changes—physical and mental—happening practically every day. Thriving on all the good food, fresh air and bracing work about the King farm, Andrew had shot up by inches.

Andrew beamed back at his father, too, seeing a tall, handsome man with dark, curly hair and a naturally distinguished air about him. The elegant, white suit Roger wore was more suited to the tropics, from which he had just come, than to Avonlea. His tanned face attested to all the time he had recently spent under the Brazilian sun.

Before Andrew and his father could so much as exchange another word, Hetty, Olivia and Alec burst upon the scene. They had all sped over from Rose Cottage as fast as their legs could carry them, and they were flushed from the effort. Alec's hat was crooked. Olivia still had her apron on. Hetty clutched her hand to her heart, as though the effect of having her favorite brother sprung upon her without warning might make her faint clean away.

"Roger!" Alec cried, rushing up. "How are you?"

"Hello, Alec."

Alec had been about to pump his younger brother's hand, but something inside him restrained the impulse and turned the gesture into a simple handshake.

Roger let go of Alec and turned to the others, his gaze flying first to his older sister.

"Hetty!"

"Welcome home, Roger," Hetty breathed, so much emotion in her voice that it cracked outright. "Goodness, it feels as if you've been gone a lifetime!"

Eyes damp, Hetty held out her hands to her brother. Roger, in a gesture of great gallantry, swept up Hetty's fingers and kissed them while Alec, behind, smothered a grimace. Roger broke off only when Olivia rushed up, flung her arms around him and kissed him soundly on the cheek.

"Olivia!" Roger laughed and hugged her back, openly indulgent towards the baby of the family.

"Roger! Oh, it's been so long," Olivia cried, her smile huge and heartfelt.

"That's quite enough sentimentality, Olivia," Hetty broke in, even though she was dabbing at tears in her own eyes. "The poor man must be exhausted. Alec, get Roger's luggage for him, will you?"

Hetty was a woman accustomed to taking control, and her order to Alec was tossed off in much the same voice she had used when telling

Felix to do Andrew's milking. She swept past her siblings and linked arms with her newly returned brother.

"Oh, no, no," Roger protested, "I'll get it."

"You will not." Hetty pointed him straight towards the house. "Alec will take care of it. Come on. Let's go inside. I'm sure Janet and Felicity will have some morsel for you to eat."

Roger had no choice but to obey, leaving Alec to deal with all the suitcases and boxes in the back of the buggy. A man did not come back from a year in South America without a mountain of baggage, observed Alec as he gritted his teeth and heaved at the most manageable-looking of the lot.

Roger started towards the house, a pronounced limp apparent in his walk. Olivia and Andrew, still smiling tremendously, trotted after. Alec, burdened with the weight of two suitcases, staggered in the rear.

"I wasn't expecting you for at least another week," Hetty told Roger affectionately, patting his wrist as if to reassure herself that he was real. "You must tell me all about Brazil. Oh, and Andrew has been my prize student all year."

Special attention from Hetty was obviously something Roger was used to, and it made him glow. He shook his head at her, his eyes dancing with all the wonderful things he had to relate.

"Oh, Hetty, it's been quite a year, and I have so many stories to tell you."

The party headed up the steps of the farmhouse and into the front hall. No sooner had they got inside than Janet King came running from the kitchen, drying her hands on her apron.

"Oh, Roger King!" she cried, flustered and overjoyed at the same time. "Oh, this is a surprise. We weren't expecting you so soon."

She immediately gathered Roger into a huge bear hug. Felicity, Cecily, Felix and Sara crowded into the hallway behind her, wide-eyed at the arrival of their uncle.

"I had to cut short my lecture tour—other obligations," Roger told Janet, while recovering from the force of her good-natured embrace.

"Well, that's our gain," Janet declared. Then she turned happily to her family. "You remember Felicity and Felix, don't you? And Cecily, our little baby. She wasn't even born when you were last here."

"Hello, Uncle Roger," Felicity said, politely shaking hands even though her eyes were wide with excitement. Felicity was very particular about her manners.

Roger stood back and looked over the crop of young Kings.

"A fine family, Alec."

"Pleased to meet you, Uncle Roger," Cecily piped up, in exact imitation of her older sister. Like all the rest, Cecily had been hearing about her Uncle Roger for ages, and now she couldn't get enough of looking at him.

"And this is Sara Stanley, Ruth's daughter," Janet said, turning to Sara, who was standing a little apart.

Ruth King had left Avonlea to marry Sara's father and had died of tuberculosis when Sara was three. Until she had come to stay with her Aunt Hetty, Sara hadn't met any of her King relatives, and certainly not her Uncle Roger.

Roger looked Sara up and down, smiles wreathing his face.

"Sara, I've read so much about you in Andrew's letters."

Sara broke into a grin and stuck out her hand, too.

"Welcome to Avonlea, Uncle Roger."

"Now this is what I call a homecoming," Roger boomed out, surrounded by just about everyone who was dear to him in the world.

Hetty had managed to get to his side again.

In the way she gazed up at him, she made it clear to everyone that Roger was the apple of her eye. She had much grander things in mind for him than a simple family get-together.

"Not at all," she informed Roger. "Your real homecoming is going to be a small reception that I'm—that we're arranging for you. You can be sure all of Avonlea will be there."

"Oh, don't go making a fuss now, Hetty," Roger said, looking a bit alarmed. Once Hetty got going on something, she really could go overboard.

"Nonsense," Hetty said breezily. "How often does this community get a chance to honor a world-famous geologist?"

Roger's face twisted into a wry smile. "Well, I wouldn't put it quite like that."

"Oh no, none of your false modesty, Roger King," chirped Hetty playfully. "You must accept what you are—a brilliant man." She paused. "Oh, goodness, that reminds me." She had been so flustered by Roger's surprise arrival that she had almost forgotten her greatest coup. "I contacted the Halifax *Herald*. They're sending a photographer and a reporter to the reception, to do a story on your accomplishments."

Roger was openly flabbergasted. Halifax was

a big city, and certainly a long way from modest, rural Prince Edward Island.

"You can't be serious!"

"I couldn't be more so," Hetty replied with a flourish, just as Alec, laden like a packhorse, panted in with another load of Roger's luggage.

"Where would you like me to put these?" he asked, wondering just how much of the luggage was actually loaded with rocks.

Roger turned and saw Alec heavily weighed down.

"Let me give you a hand."

"Oh no," insisted Janet, with complete disregard for her husband's back, "that's all right. I'll show Alec where it goes."

Ignoring Alec, Hetty took Roger by the elbow again.

"You poor thing. You must be famished! Now, hear that, Janet? We must feed our conquering hero."

"Papa," said Andrew ecstatically, putting his arm around his father, and with that, the little group set off towards the kitchen, leaving Alec to deal with the baggage.

Janet, pausing behind, bent close to her husband. Her expression now exactly mirrored that on Alec's face.

"I tell you, Alec," she whispered through her teeth, "if I have to listen to one more minute of Hetty's adoration, I'm going to be sick to my stomach!"

Alec managed a feeble grin in response and struggled up the stairs as Janet swept out of the hall.

Sara Stanley now saw a chance to get the answer to some questions of her own. Just outside the kitchen, she pulled her Aunt Olivia discreetly aside.

"Aunt Olivia, what happened to Uncle Roger's leg?" Observant child that she was, she had noticed Roger's limp

"Oh," said Olivia quickly, "he fell and hurt it when he was a little baby."

"How?"

"Oh, Sara, it happened a long time ago. Don't say anything about it, please." Olivia's imploring look squelched the rest of the questions on Sara's lips.

Chapter Six

Supper that evening around the huge kitchen table of the farmhouse proved a jolly occasion to be sure. With everyone laughing and talking and trying to get a word in edgewise, there was hardly time to eat, although Felix did his best to put away a large share of the food.

Afterward, Alec and Janet thought they were never going to get Hetty out the door. But, eventually, even Hetty had to go home, accompanied by Olivia and Sara. When the King children were finally in bed, Alec, Janet and Roger had the kitchen to themselves and remained there until late, chatting comfortably. Eventually, however, Roger began to look restless and preoccupied.

"All I need is a quiet corner to finish this report," he was saying, as he polished off what was, he fervently hoped, his final cup of tea of the day.

Janet, standing behind him, cleared away the cup and a plate now empty of her home-baked oatmeal cookies. Roger always had been a bear for work, she remembered.

"Oh, well, what about the parlor, Alec?"

"Certainly. No one will bother you there," Alec said agreeably, beckoning to Roger. "Come on."

Leaving Janet behind to clear up, the two men rose from the table and left the kitchen. Alec grinned as they stepped through the wide doors to the parlor—the best room of the house, reserved for important occasions and formal tea with visitors.

"Remember the time you threw your book at me and broke that window?"

"Father was so mad, he almost twisted both our ears off!" Roger chuckled slowly. "This room sure brings back a lot of memories."

He stood a moment, looking around at the familiar flowered wallpaper, the polished sideboard, the portraits of King ancestors in their heavy wooden frames.

"I must have spent half my childhood in here studying," Roger said, a strange, unreadable note in his voice.

"It certainly paid off," Alec returned affably, thinking of how important his brother had become.

Roger wasn't listening. He went over to the window and stared pensively into the night, holding the lace curtain back with one hand. Now that he was a man, he guessed how unnatural it had been for a boy on a farm to spend so much of his time at a shiny parlor table poring over books.

"Sometimes I'd put away the books and come over here just to watch you and the others play hockey down at the pond."

Now Alec looked uneasy, glancing at his brother's lame leg.

"Aw! You'd have just frozen your feet, like the rest of us."

Roger looked as though he would have been very glad to freeze his feet with the rest of them, if only he had been able. The corner of his mouth twisted down.

"At least I would have had a choice...if it hadn't been for my bad leg."

Roger let the curtain drop again, as upon his own childhood, and turned to the table. Urgent business awaited and he must get straight to it.

He crossed to the table and opened a leather case, from which he removed a sheaf of papers. He was unaware that Andrew, dressed in a plaid dressing gown and carrying a lamp, had slipped down the stairs and was waiting at the door.

Andrew hadn't seen his father for so long, he could barely stand to spend a minute away from him, much less be expected to spend the whole night in a bedroom asleep. He had waited up for just this moment, when he might speak to his father alone. As soon as he felt sure that he wouldn't be interrupting, he padded in, the lamp in one hand and the ever-present fishing basket in the other.

When Alec saw the hungry way the boy eyed his father, he smiled a little to himself and turned back towards the parlor door.

"Ah, Andrew! I'm sure you and your father have lots to talk about. I'll just leave you to it." Alec understood a lot about boys, perhaps much more than Roger.

As Alec went out, Roger sat down and started leafing through his pile of papers. This wasn't exactly the greeting Andrew had expected. Quickly, he came closer, hefting the fishing basket.

"I was hoping you could take a look at my rock collection."

Roger lifted his head from the papers spread out around him and glanced up at Andrew.

"Just let me finish unpacking my papers, son."

"Aunt Hetty told me about the collection you had when you were my age," Andrew said eagerly. "She's saved all sorts of things of yours, and I—"

"Oh, now that reminds me." Roger reached to the bottom of his briefcase and came up with something wrapped in soft cloth. "I brought this for you, son."

As Andrew unfolded the cloth, a piece of

rock, glinting richly in the lamplight, was revealed. Andrew gazed at it, much impressed.

"Thanks," he breathed, delighted with such a dazzling gift.

"It's ore, laced with gold."

"Gold!" Andrew declared. "You sure don't find that around here."

Roger, who should have been sharing his son's pleasure, was paying more attention to his briefcase.

"Ah," he muttered, distracted, "here it is." He pulled a fat folder from the case and started to arrange it on the table beside the rest of the papers. "The company's still having trouble with that smelter I developed for them."

Doubt, suspicion and just a touch of alarm crept into Andrew's eyes.

"I thought that...well, your contract *is* finished with them, isn't it?"

Roger stroked his chin thoughtfully before answering.

"Well, technically, yes. Perhaps these changes I'm preparing will alleviate some of their troubles."

In an effort to make his presence truly felt, Andrew lifted up the fishing basket and set it on top of his father's papers.

"Well, could you just take a look at—?"

Roger put a restraining hand on the basket handle, preventing Andrew from opening the lid.

"Now, look, Andrew...I really must get started on this analysis," he said quickly. "I cut short my tour so that I could respond to this immediately. Perhaps we could look at your collection later."

Disappointment spread over Andrew's face even though he strove manfully to hide it.

"I understand. If you're that busy, then..."

"We'll look at it in the morning," Roger promised, flipping the folder open. "Good night, now, son. It's awfully good to see you again."

Andrew looked as though he were beginning to have his doubts about this last statement. He could see his father already had his mind on finishing the report.

"All right," he murmured hesitantly. "Good night."

Roger patted Andrew's shoulder absently and turned to organize his work. Crestfallen, Andrew trudged slowly out of the parlor, toting his rock collection and the lighted lamp he had brought down with him.

Andrew was about to head up the stairs just

as his Uncle Alec was coming down. Seeing the boy, Alec paused in surprise. He had expected the private father-son reunion to go on merrily far into the night.

"Off to bed so soon?"

Andrew dropped his head.

"Father's got a lot of urgent work to attend to."

Ah, so that was the way the wind blew. Alec nodded, doing his best to look comforting and wise.

"Well, when the pressure's off, he'll...he'll have more time to spend with you."

"I guess," Andrew mumbled.

"Things'll get back to normal."

Without answering, Andrew plodded on up the stairs, hauling the old fishing basket. "Bunch of dumb rocks," he muttered as he reached the landing. Alec turned at the foot of the stairs and watched with concern as the dejected boy disappeared down the dark hallway and into his room.

Chapter Seven

Roger King worked late into the night on his report, so late that no one heard him finally go up to bed. He had his breakfast by himself the next morning and emerged from the front door of the farmhouse to find Alec loading bags into the back of the buggy.

"Off to town, Alec?" Roger asked, blinking in the sunshine.

Roger was in his shirtsleeves and vest, unhampered by collar or necktie. Alec smiled, glad to see him finally looking as though he were at home.

"Sure am. You care to join me?"

Alec's invitation was genuine. He really would relish a pleasant drive into Avonlea with his newly returned brother at his side. Roger, still preoccupied, only held out an envelope.

"Sorry, another time. Would you mind posting this letter for me?"

The envelope looked important, as did all Roger's correspondence. With a sigh, Alec took the letter and climbed up into the driver's seat.

"You finish all your work last night?"

Wearily, Roger shook his head. "No, no, just some preliminary recommendations."

"I see," said Alec, gathering up the reins. Then he paused, thinking of the boyish figure he had seen forlornly climbing the stairs last night. "Have you seen Andrew this morning?"

"No." Roger shook his head. "Must still be doing his chores."

As Roger turned to go, Alec shifted round on the seat and gathered up the reins. If he couldn't have his brother's company this morning, perhaps something could be made of the afternoon.

"Roger, I was...uh...I was thinking maybe we could take Felix and Andrew over to the auction in Carmody this afternoon," he suggested.

"I would have thought you had plenty to do around here."

Looking faintly pained at Roger's tone, Alec shrugged.

"Oh, nothing that can't wait till tomorrow. Might do us all a world of good to take a few hours off, clear our heads, see some old friends. You know, the auctioneer up there is Hugh Macdonald. You remember—"

"My work won't wait, Alec," Roger ground out, cutting his brother off.

Alec's mouth tightened. After all, he thought the family was only just together after months and months apart. It seemed a shame to waste such a fine opportunity.

"It's just...well, such a pleasant day...I mean, I know Andrew would enjoy it."

For some reason, Roger seemed to grow progressively more annoyed with everything Alec said. He slid a hand into his pocket.

"Still trying to play my big brother, aren't you?" he tossed out with a sharpness that took Alec completely off guard.

Shocked, Alec drew in a breath, ready to argue. Then, seeing his brother's stubborn expression, Alec shut his mouth again in the interests of keeping the peace. "Never mind," was all he said before he clucked to the horse and drove off.

Roger stood in front of the farmhouse, staring after Alec until the buggy disappeared from sight around the bend. Then, sighing, he went back to the parlor and his waiting report.

Trying to ignore this first small cloud a shadow over the family harmony, Alec drove briskly on to Avonlea. Yet no sooner had he rattled over the covered bridge into the village itself than trouble descended upon him again— this time in the form of Amos Spry. Amos spotted the buggy rolling over the bridge and chased after it awkwardly.

"Alec! Alec!" he called out, his face the very picture of distress.

Hearing his name, Alec stopped the horse and twisted around in his seat.

"Morning, Amos. How's the crop coming?"

Amos ran till he caught up with the buggy.

"You haven't heard the news, have you?" he asked sorrowfully, looking as though he might start beating his own breast.

"News? What's that?"

"There was a run on the Abbey Bank in Carmody yesterday. The Abbey made some bad investments out West...lost a lot of money. When folks got wind the bank was in trouble, they rushed to take their money out. So they called in all their loans."

Alec looked perfectly astonished. The King family kept their money in the Abbey Bank. It had always been considered as safe as a vault.

"A bank run?"

A bank's wealth, the money it lent and invested, the money that made it secure, was really only the sum total of all the accounts ordinary people kept there. If the ordinary people suddenly got nervous about a bank's security and rushed to draw their money out, why, then the bank could go stone broke in a matter of days. If even a small bank run caused a bank's coffers to get too low, then it was natural that the bank would call in its loans so as to have the money on hand in case of further emergency.

Amos didn't really care about the bank's troubles; he cared about his own—his own and Alec King's. Biting his lips nervously, he broke the worst of the news to Alec.

"They called in my loan, and they seized your money!"

"No!" cried Alec in disbelief.

Amos's head sank down. He appeared utterly wretched and he flung out his hands in defeat.

"Alec, I don't know what to say. I told you— everything I touch goes sour. I'm sorry."

Alec simply sat in the buggy seat for a moment, trying to absorb what he had just heard. Since he had guaranteed Amos's loan, the bank would have simply taken the money out of the King account to make good for what Amos owed. Bad as things looked, Alec groped quickly for something positive to say. He knew he had to brace Amos's spirits or the King money might be swallowed up for good.

"Well, it's not all lost, Amos," he responded, doing his best not to seem rattled. "You've still got your crop. You can repay me when you get it in. I'll be over in the morning to give you a hand."

"Yeah."

The word was barely audible to Alec. He drove off, leaving Amos only half convinced that anything good could ever happen to him again.

Back at the King farm, Roger was having trouble concentrating on his report. Somehow the technical problems of a mining operation in Brazil seemed impossibly far away from the tall grass, high breeze and golden sun on a small farm in Prince Edward Island.

Roger decided that he had better take a break from his paperwork in order to look around the family farm with an eye to making improvements. After all, he was the educated one in the family, and he'd seen a lot more of the world than Alec had ever dreamed of. What better place to apply all this experience than right there at home?

Wearing an old smock coat, and with a brimmed hat perched on his head, Roger took himself on a grand tour. In the potato field, he grasped a handful of earth, looking at it thoughtfully and letting it trickle away through his fingers. Then he wandered around checking the fences, fiddling with the farm machinery and poking about in the barn.

As he went, he periodically opened up his

notebook and wrote in it. The notations he had made so far read:

New fencing
Larger dairy herd
Crop rotation
Irrigation system.

When he'd added the word "Mechanization" to the list, he closed the notebook and walked back to the house. The gleam in his eye indicated that he meant to show his brother a thing or two about the modern world.

Alec, meanwhile, had his own troubles with the business of farming. When he got back from Avonlea, he called the family together in the big farmhouse kitchen for a meeting. The kitchen was already a hive of pie-baking activity. Janet, Felicity and Sara had been pressed into service to prepare for Hetty's reception. Pie plates filled with dough covered the table, and Sara was hard at work peeling apples for the filling. Andrew and Felix had just brought in another bushel of apples when Hetty and Olivia bustled in.

"Alec, what is all this about?" Hetty demanded. "I'm extremely busy. A reception of this magnitude doesn't organize itself, you know."

Hetty's eye fell on the waiting pie crusts,

which immediately reminded her how much still had to be done to prepare food for the big event. She turned distractedly to her sister.

"Oh, good heavens, Olivia. I hope Janet remembered to get the...uh..."

"...pickled preserves," Hetty and Olivia ended up saying in unison.

Hetty looked around for Janet, who was supposed to be supervising the pie-making operations.

"Where is she, anyway?"

"She's lying down," Alec told her, glancing towards the stairs.

This last pregnancy seemed to be taking a lot out of Janet, making her tired in the middle of the day and shortening her patience with household problems. It was just as well, Alec thought, that she wasn't there to hear what he had to say.

"This will just take a minute," he began, addressing everyone at once and plunging straight into his topic. "Amos Spry has broken his arm, and I've offered to give him a hand with his crops, so, for the next few weeks, I'll be working at his place."

Hetty was one of those in Avonlea who had a low opinion of the Sprys. She gave a loud sniff of disapproval.

"Giving help to Amos Spry is a complete and utter waste of time," she declared.

"Hetty, that's unkind," protested Olivia, who was about as tenderhearted as it was possible to be.

Hetty only sniffed louder. "You can't make a silk purse out of a sow's ear. I mean, really, I—"

"Hetty, please." Alec raised his hand to cut off her tirade. "Now, I can't possibly work both farms, so...there's gonna be a lot more work around here for everyone else."

Andrew sighed, and Felix looked disgusted, knowing who was going to get a generous helping of the extra work.

As Alec finished speaking, Roger strolled into the room, the report he was working on in his hand. He had been listening from the parlor doorway.

"I'm still busy with my report," Roger interjected, "but I'm sure I can spare some time to help keep an eye on things around here for you."

"Oh, thanks, Roger," Alec said, surprised and pleased, thinking that his brother wanted to make up for snapping at him earlier in the day.

Roger had other motives in mind, however. In fact, he was delighted to get his chance to supervise the farm.

"Actually," Roger proceeded, "I've noticed a

few aspects of your operation that could be made more efficient."

The pleasure faded from Alec's face as he recognized his brother's lecturing tone. Roger could sound very much like Hetty, especially when he imagined he was imparting superior information. Things on the home front, Alec reflected as he braced himself inwardly, could very easily become as troublesome as the problems with Amos Spry.

Chapter Eight

In spite of Hetty's objections, Amos Spry came to pick up Alec early the next morning. As the two men rode along in the buggy, Amos expressed his appreciation—and his misgivings.

"I hope all your help's not going to waste, Alec," he said nervously, looking gloomier than ever in the morning sunshine.

Alec glanced over his shoulder towards the King farm somewhat ruefully, then chuckled. What he'd started, he certainly meant to finish, Hetty or no Hetty. The only way the Kings were going to get their money back was to see every last potato on the Spry land dug up and hauled profitably to market.

"Have no fear, Amos," Alec said heartily. "We'll get your crop in."

At the same time, Roger was limping along the path to Rose Cottage. He had his notebook in his hand and purpose etched on his face. If he had his way, improvements were going to arrive at the King farm so quickly that Alec's head would spin!

When Roger stepped into the parlor, he found Hetty at her desk, long lists laid out in front of her. She was frowning in deep concentration and counting out, under her breath, the number of guests she had invited to the reception.

"Hetty," Roger called out, stamping in. "Have you got a minute?"

Though she felt she scarcely had a second to spare, Hetty willingly stopped work at once. She might have snapped at anyone else for interrupting her, but she always had plenty of time for Roger.

"For you, always." She smiled. "Go on, sit yourself down. I was just working on plans for your reception. Nothing that can't wait, of course."

"I've been taking some time to look at Alec's operations," said Roger, energetically. "Now, he's a good farmer, but he's such a slave to traditional methods."

"Wouldn't surprise me, though I do try not to get involved with what Alec does on the farm," Hetty replied, with a wave that seemed to dismiss all Alec's hard-won knowledge.

Roger slid forward to the edge of his chair and regarded Hetty meaningfully.

"Well, perhaps you should. He works your land, too, after all. And the farm belongs to the whole family, through the family trust. We all share in the profits, don't we?"

"Well, yes...I suppose." Hetty shrugged. It wasn't a matter that she generally concerned herself with.

"Then we both have a vested interest in what goes on here," Roger continued, firmly drawing her into his plans.

"Well, yes, of course," Hetty admitted, frowning a little but ready to agree with anything her brother said. "It *is* our farm, too. What are you suggesting?"

Pulling the notebook from his pocket, Roger flipped through it until he came to the pages now covered with rows of crisp notations. At the same time, he treated Hetty to a conspiratorial smile.

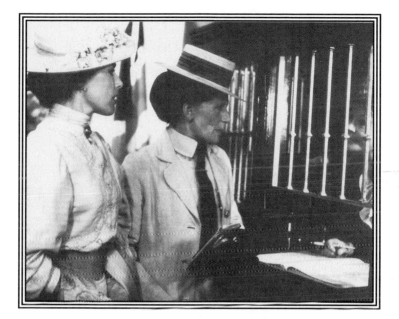

❧❧❧

"Two dollars and fifty cents?" Hetty squawked.
"Well, there must be a mistake!"

❧❧❧

"It's only a picture," Olivia whispered,
in an effort to comfort Andrew.

❧❧❧

"What did you do that for?
You stuck-up little Hetty's pet!"
Vengefully, Felix flew at Andrew, trying to grab a
handful of his cousin's hair.

ↃↄↃↄↃↄ

Alec was tired of Roger and Hetty's dramatics.
"Look, we've got a cow in there that
might die if I don't get a vet."

"Maybe," he suggested slowly, "it's time we nudged Alec into the modern world."

"MacCRAE BROTHERS AGRICULTURAL EQUIPMENT, MARKDALE, P.E.I." read Andrew aloud as he watched the large crate being hauled into Alec's barn. Now, Andrew waited in anticipation as he watched his father pry it open. They'd been waiting more than a week for the delivery. When the last nail came loose, the whole side of the crate fell away, revealing a complicated-looking machine inside.

"Strange-looking contraption, isn't it?" Andrew commented. Though he was puzzled by the shiny bowls and the pump with a handle on it, all nested carefully in packing straw, he was more than prepared to admire anything his father thought the farm should have.

"Yes, indeed," laughed Roger, even as he spotted Hetty on the march towards them. "The most modern milking machine there is."

"Roger!" Hetty called out. "Roger, this telegram just arrived for you."

She held out the bright yellow envelope, which Roger calmly took as though he were accustomed to receiving telegrams every day.

"Thank you."

As Roger set about tearing open the envelope, Hetty stepped over to the open crate and peered at the contents. When she realized what it was, she pressed her hands together in satisfaction.

"Oh, oh, isn't this wonderful?" she exclaimed, even though she couldn't tell one end of the contraption from the other.

Andrew, ignoring Hetty, had his eyes riveted on his father and the telegram.

"Where's it from?" he wanted to know, already feeling apprehensive.

Hetty, while still examining the milking machine, was also keeping an eye on Roger's changing expression. In her experience, telegrams were usually connected with emergencies of the most inconvenient sort.

"Not bad news, I hope," she ventured, for Roger was reading quickly, his brow furrowed, the corners of his mouth drawn in.

"It's the mining project."

Now a look of panic touched Andrew. "You don't have to go, do you?" he asked, his voice growing small. South America was such a long, long way away.

Roger was saved from answering by the arrival of Alec and Felix on the scene. Alec was worn out after a long day at Amos Spry's, and it showed on his face. The first thing Alec spotted was Roger and Hetty with their heads together. The second thing he spotted was the crate.

"All right, what are you up to?" he asked warily as he bent down to look into the crate. "What the heck's this thing?"

"Hetty and I thought it was time you came out of the Dark Ages and adopted more progressive farming techniques," Roger told his older brother calmly, tucking the telegram into his back pocket.

Alec stared at his brother, then at the milking machine, then laughed aloud in disbelief.

"We can't afford a milking machine," he shot back. "Besides, these things may work in theory, but they've been nothing but trouble for dairy farmers."

Just as Hetty had suspected, Alec was going to object. Providing reinforcement, Hetty positioned herself stoutly at Roger's side.

"Now, don't fret, Alec. I've already paid for it. Yes, out of the King trust account."

"Oh."

For no reason anyone could fathom, Alec lapsed rather abruptly into silence. Roger took this as a victory for modernization and pressed his advantage.

"Alec, we are living in changing times," Roger declaimed expansively, and with more than a little condescension towards his brother. "Technology is revolutionizing the lives we lead, both in the city and the country. If you fail to keep up, you simply won't survive."

"We only have three cows, Uncle Roger," Felix piped up, getting straight to the point.

"Exactly," Roger replied, as if this made his argument. "What you need is twenty or thirty."

"Twenty or thirty!" Felix shuddered at the very thought. All he could imagine was himself spending the rest of his childhood trying to milk them.

"It's not a dairy operation I'm running, Roger," Alec added, having found his voice again and making a visible effort to keep cool.

"You have to specialize in order to turn a reasonable profit," Roger replied, again with that patronizing air of the expert addressing the untutored. "You have to look at the farm as a business."

Hetty, determined not to be left out of this glorious march into the future, added her voice to the chorus.

"Roger and I have been discussing plans to improve the entire—"

"Now hold your horses, you two," Alec burst

out, unable to believe his ears. "I run this farm. You could at least include me in these discussions."

"Don't be silly, Alec," his sister said dismissively. "You would never have agreed to it."

Mottled red began to climb up Alec's neck. He was struggling hard to control his rising temper.

"Well, if you two are such experts in agriculture, maybe *you* should run the farm."

"Well, maybe we *should* be running this farm," Roger shot back bluntly, as much as saying out loud that Alec was hopelessly behind the times.

Now Alec exploded completely. He jerked away from the crate and shook his finger forcefully at his brother.

"Let's get something straight here, Roger. You got the education, I got the farm. Now I don't interfere in your affairs, so don't you meddle in mine."

With that salvo fired, Alec turned on his heel and strode off towards the house, leaving the little group temporarily speechless.

Felix, ever loyal to his father, immediately set out to follow. But before he went, he marched over to Andrew. "I think he means it," he muttered. Then he quickly sped off out of the barn.

Chapter Nine

Alec King was generally such a steady, easygoing fellow that it took a few seconds for Roger to realize that his brother was truly offended. He started out at once towards the farmhouse in pursuit, making much slower progress than Alec because of his bad leg. It had been very foolish, Roger realized, to make Alec angry—especially in view of what Roger now had to ask.

In the farmhouse kitchen, Alec was pouring himself a glass of water from the pitcher and glowering at the wall. Advancing into this stony silence, broken only by the ticking of the clock, Roger now did his best to sound conciliatory.

"Listen, Alec," he began from the doorway, "I really was only trying to help. You're too stubborn for your own good sometimes."

Alec took another swallow from the water glass, as though he needed to douse the words burning in his throat.

"I appreciate your concern," he answered coolly, "but we're managing."

Roger limped further into the kitchen and stood just on the other side of the broad kitchen table. He looked worried, but about more than just the new milking machine.

"I never doubted that," Roger told his brother in a placating voice. "You know, you've never listened to any voice other than your own, and probably rightly so, so I will keep my nose out of your affairs in future. As it stands, I won't be here much longer anyway."

"Oh?" Surprised by Roger's sudden capitulation, Alec finally put down the glass and faced his brother. It wasn't like Roger to give in so easily.

"I must return to Brazil," Roger said slowly, as if breaking the news to himself as well as his brother.

This bombshell crashed into the stillness. Alec, once he got over the surprise, began to frown.

"Does Andrew know about this?" he asked, his first concern being for the boy's disappointment.

"No."

Roger paused and then, a little hesitantly, put forward his request.

"Would you be amenable to keeping Andrew here at Avonlea for another year?"

A year! That was an eon in the life of a growing boy. And Andrew had already spent one year away from his father. Alec tugged at the bib of his overalls, looking grave.

"I don't think that's a good idea, Roger. He's been looking forward to being with you for a long time."

"I know that, Alec." Roger sighed. "But I feel I have a moral obligation to complete this job satisfactorily."

"What about your responsibility to your son?" Alec demanded, severely.

Alec had had a lot more experience with children than Roger, and he realized the damage that a further separation could inflict on Andrew. Probably, in his heart, Roger suspected it too, for he suddenly bristled all over, going on the attack so that he wouldn't have to really think about what another trip to Brazil would mean for his son.

"You're a fine one to talk about responsibilities," Roger shot back, a patronizing tone creeping in once again, "running around taking care of a neighbor's problems when you should be at home running this place."

With great self-restraint, Alec refused to take the bait. His efforts on behalf of Amos Spry were not the point here.

"I'm just thinking of what's best for Andrew," he responded patiently.

Roger began to pace the kitchen, growing

agitated and angry as Alec tried to tell him things he really didn't want to hear.

"I'm not working for my own glory. I'm working for my son's security," Roger rasped, as though that justified everything he did.

There were other, more important, forms of security for children than money, Alec thought. The greatest security of all was having a loving parent always close by. Seeing Roger bent on his course of action, Alec could only sigh.

"He's going to be very disappointed."

Roger remained unmoved, his face set. "I know Andrew better than anyone else," he replied. "He'll understand."

Alec certainly had his doubts about that, but he saw that further argument with Roger would be futile. Picking up his cap, Alec went out the side door and back to work. He didn't see Andrew, walking dejectedly towards the house, kicking at the dirt as he went and taking an angry whack at the empty tree swing.

Andrew came into the house and found his father in the sun room. As usual, Roger was surrounded by papers and all wrapped up in his report. Andrew just stood in the door watching this scene, anger and disappointment struggling on his face as he waited for his father to notice him.

"Huh..." Roger grunted, at last aware of the lad's presence.

"You have to go back to Brazil, don't you?" Andrew flung out reproachfully.

The bald question caught Roger completely unprepared. He had forgotten how perceptive Andrew was and, also, that the boy had seen too many telegrams in his life not to know the meaning of them. Roger's papers slid from his hands as he scrambled to explain himself, guilty and uncomfortable because he hadn't expected to have to face this issue so soon.

"I was going to talk to you about that," he said clumsily. "It's only for another year. It's not really a long time, now, is it?"

To Andrew, right then, it seemed like a century stretching ahead of him, a lonely tunnel with no end in sight. Yet he also saw how important it was to his father to go, and how much his father wanted him to say it was all right. The entreating words Andrew had been about to say died in his throat. He would only upset his father further if he started to argue now.

"No, I guess not," Andrew managed, staring down at the floor.

"I knew you'd understand, son," Roger said

in swift satisfaction. He was so relieved that the matter had been dealt with easily that he failed to see the bitter disappointment in his son's eyes.

Roger almost turned back to his report, but then he stopped himself. Perhaps he could find a moment or two to spend with the boy. He beamed, suddenly remembering one of Andrew's interests.

"Whatever happened to that rock collection you wanted to show me?" he asked genially.

But Andrew could play the waiting game, too. He turned away, his throat tight. The very last thing he wanted, right then, was his father throwing him a sop of attention as a reward for not making a fuss about Brazil.

"Perhaps later. I have other things to do."

Roger raised his eyebrows in faint surprise, and then shrugged. "Later it is," he murmured, already immersed once more in his report.

Casting a somber backward glance, Andrew went to the door. He paused there, his hand on the frame, then turned around as though he suddenly meant to express his real feelings. All he saw, though, was the back of his father's head as he bent over the table again, completely engrossed in his work. Lonely boys and their problems seemed to be a million miles away from Roger's thoughts. Sadly, Andrew slipped his cap back on and silently left the room.

By the time Andrew had scuffed his shoes all the way over to the barn, his sadness had turned to a kind of seething anger. Oblivious to the chores awaiting him, he leaned against the stone foundation and fired pebbles, one after the other, at the ground a few yards from his feet. Felix, who had been sweating in the hayfield again, came into the barnyard and spotted Andrew's idleness. Steamed up—and having never forgotten about the fishing basket, of course—Felix came marching over.

"You haven't milked one cow yet," he hissed scornfully. "What would you and your father do with thirty?"

"Why don't you squeal a little louder, you little tattletale," Andrew shot back, in a dangerous mood.

This only made Felix more determined to vent his spleen upon his cousin. His lip curled. "Your father and his fancy ideas!"

"What do you know?" Andrew muttered blackly, shooting a pebble far too close to Felix's toes.

"I know I want my fishing basket back!" Felix flared, fixing upon his major grievance and stepping close enough to thrust his jaw into Andrew's face.

"Well, it's not yours." Andrew stood up and gave Felix a good push backward to emphasize the humiliating fact.

"It is so!"

Planting his boots in the dirt, Felix shoved vigorously back.

Andrew, full of turmoil inside, was ready for a fight. His palms thudded into Felix's chest, sending Felix staggering. Ducking his head in fury, Felix charged, ready to slam Andrew into the stone foundation of the barn. He would have succeeded had Alec not stepped out of the stable at that moment and grasped each boy by the nape of the neck.

"WHOA! Hey, hey, hey! What's all this about?"

"Andrew hasn't milked the cows yet," Felix announced, choosing the sin most likely to rile his father.

"Why don't you keep your nose out of other people's business?" Andrew yelled at Felix, and he would have shoved his cousin again had it not been for Alec's large hand gripping his shoulder.

"Well," Felix jeered, not giving up, "it's way past milking time."

Alec could see there was more than chore-shirking going on here. He released the boys and stood back.

"That's enough, Felix. You go and feed the chickens."

Seeing he was going to get no backup from his father, Felix turned and dashed away, both his hands balled into fists. Alec turned back to Andrew, guessing very well what must have passed between the boy and his own father.

"Andrew, I...well, I understand why you're upset."

"I'm not upset," Andrew replied stubbornly, glaring straight ahead, his face a mask.

Alec realized there was no point talking to the boy right then. The hurt was too fresh and Andrew too wrought up. What Andrew needed was a good physical distraction, which Alec could certainly provide.

"Well, then you can do your chores, right?"

Alec grabbed a milk pail from the wall and handed it to Andrew, who took it and walked sullenly away. Alec watched him leave, misery apparent in every limb. Then, shaking his head, Alec went back into the barn to finish unharnessing the horse.

Chapter Ten

Hetty pressed on relentlessly with her plans for Roger's reception. She sent invitations, planned refreshments that grew more grandiose with each passing day, commandeered teacups, worried about the weather and generally drove most of the Kings to distraction with her constant flurry.

"The people of Avonlea are certainly going to remember Roger King's reception if I have anything to do with it," Hetty asserted firmly and often, running her eye over her numerous and ever-present lists.

And, of course, she soon discovered that such a major social event was going to cost her money—money that she would have to get out of the King trust account at the Abbey Bank. Straightaway, she and Olivia set out to Carmody to make the necessary withdrawal.

Because of the number of errands on their list for the day, they had to stop at the bank during one of its busiest times. They nodded to people they knew as they joined the line waiting to be served at the teller's wicket. Even then, there was no safety from Hetty's lists. In the bank lineup, Hetty whipped one from her bag and began to go over it with Olivia.

Olivia sighed and kept her thoughts to herself. The Kings, at least, would never forget this occasion—provided they had any strength left after all the work Hetty was putting them through.

The woman ahead of Hetty finished her business and left. Stuffing her list away, Hetty stepped up to the wicket to take her turn. She handed the teller her account card. The teller was a plump, gray-haired woman who had an ear-trumpet lying on the counter by her side.

"Good afternoon," Hetty greeted her. "I wish to withdraw forty dollars from this account."

"Thirty, did you say?" asked the teller, who was more than a little deaf. She lifted up the ear-trumpet and aimed it at Hetty.

"No, four-ty," Hetty repeated, enunciating the number sharply into the wide end of the device.

Nodding, the teller set down the trumpet, entered the debit and handed Hetty her money.

"Sign here, please," the teller asked, pushing forward the account book.

"Mm-hmm," Hetty murmured as she picked up the pen and signed with a flourish, demonstrating the beautiful penmanship of which she was so justly proud.

"And that brings your balance to two dollars and fifty cents," the teller said matter-of-factly. "Next, please."

"Thank you very much," Hetty murmured, smiling and turning to leave. Since her mind had been on the reception the whole time, she took three steps towards the door before the teller's words actually sank in. Jerking to a halt, she spun round and pushed her way back to the teller's window. In her haste, she all but knocked over the woman next in line, who had just taken her place at the grille.

"Two dollars and fifty cents?" Hetty squawked. "Well, there must be a mistake!"

"A what?" The teller held up her ear-trumpet again, the better to catch Hetty's words.

"A mistake," Hetty sputtered, trying to keep her voice down.

Already, the customers in line behind her were starting to look interested. And in Avonlea, no delicious little piece of gossip was ever overlooked.

"There's no mistake, madam," the teller announced loudly. "Your balance is two dollars and fifty cents. Next, please."

Casting a glance behind her, Hetty leaned over and whispered forcefully into the teller's ear-trumpet. "My good woman, there has to be a substantial amount of money in this account. It is the King trust account. Clearly, you have confused our number with somebody else's. Kindly check it again."

The teller shook the ear-trumpet irritably. "Why are you whispering? I can barely hear you when you're talking, let alone whispering."

"I said," Hetty growled, finally bursting into a shout, *"check it again!"*

Realizing how loud she had just been, Hetty shut her mouth firmly and looked studiously away from the others. The teller turned to the ledger while Olivia twisted at her handbag, looking very uncomfortable.

"Oh, good Lord," the teller said, mildly shocked, "I did make a mistake. I'm so glad you pressed me to check. I would have been," she added under her breath as the manager peered out of his office behind her, "in a good deal of hot water."

Vindicated, Hetty smiled in anticipation of a fat balance statement.

"Your balance isn't two dollars and fifty cents," the teller informed Hetty breathlessly. "It's one dollar and fifty cents."

Hetty could only stare at the teller and gasp faintly. "What did you say?"

The teller was only too happy to repeat the sum—and in the hearing of a whole bank full of customers. This time Hetty could not argue, for there the figures were, in black and white, down in the account book. The bulk of the money had already been withdrawn—under Alec King's signature!

As fast as she could, Olivia rushed Hetty out into the fresh air to fan her with her handkerchief. The only bright side to this disaster, Olivia thought distractedly as she watched Hetty turn a furious crimson, was that, for once, the lists for the reception were forgotten.

As soon as Hetty recovered her powers of locomotion, she went charging straight to the King farm, stinging from the embarrassment in the bank line, not to mention the worry about what had happened to the healthy bank balance. Perhaps Alec had had a fit of madness from eating oysters out of season? Or the Kings had been the victims of a forger dressed up like Alec who had bamboozled that silly, deaf teller?

Hetty charged past the cows grazing peacefully in the fields and over to the barn where Alec, all unsuspecting, was cleaning out the stables. By the time Hetty sailed up to him, she was accompanied by Roger, whom she had made sure to collect in her wake.

"Alec!" she shouted. "Alec King. I have just returned from the bank in Carmody, and the teller tells me the money's gone. Good grief, Alec, what have you done with the money?"

Here came the trouble Alec had fervently hoped to avoid. Until Amos Spry got paid for his crop, Alec had hoped none of his family would look too closely at the King bank account. Now, Alec had no choice but to set down his shovel and take on the look of a man caught openly in crime.

"Well, I...I'm sorry, Hetty. I meant to explain earlier."

"Explain what?" Hetty demanded blazingly.

Alec let out a sigh and rubbed at his arm. "It's a long story. You see, Amos Spry needed—"

"Are you actually saying you gave that money to Amos Spry?" Hetty exploded, everything about her, right up to her quivering hat feathers, expressing her outraged disbelief.

"I'm sure we'll get the money back," Alec told her, trying his best to sound soothing.

No amount of soothing was going to pacify Hetty. Once she got a bee in her bonnet, life was apt to be miserable for everybody until she, somehow, got it out again. Now here she was, every minute acting more and more like a volcano about to erupt.

"Why didn't you just take it out of the bank and burn it?!" she cried, growing even more violently red.

"That money belongs to all of us—" Roger put in. He was nearly as irate as Hetty and even more determined to berate Alec for his idiocy. "—Olivia, Hetty, me—"

"Amos's crop's worth twice what I lent him. He'll repay," Alec insisted, feeling besieged.

Hetty certainly didn't think much of that prospect. "Oh, we'll never see that money again. Alec King, you're an irresponsible fool." Hetty turned on her heel to leave, certain that Alec had just brought ruin upon them all.

"You'll get your money back, Hetty," Alec called out to her as she stormed away. "I know what I'm doing."

He looked in appeal to his brother, but Roger was stoutly on Hetty's side, unable to resist the chance to get in one more potshot at Alec's supposed incompetence.

"Oh, and I suppose handing all that money over to the likes of the Sprys shows your good business sense?"

He paused, and then, through his teeth, he flung what must have been a boyhood taunt at Alec.

"You can't do anything right."

As his brother and sister marched away, Alec leaned on the manure shovel looking quite defeated. Families were supposed to stick together, to help each other, he thought, not work a fellow over with brickbats and leave him stranded on the edge of the manure pile. Alec tossed down the shovel and went in search of consolation. Hetty and Roger might be against him, but surely he could get some support from his wife.

In the kitchen, Janet had plenty of problems of her own. That evening the kitchen table was completely covered with the freshly baked pies and cakes for the reception the very next day. Dessert-making was the job Hetty had unloaded on Janet and Felicity. The two had slaved in the kitchen, roasting in the heat blasting out from the cook stove as batch after batch went into the oven to be baked. Now, at the end of an exhausting day, when the children were finally in bed, Janet was counting anxiously, trying to calculate whether, at long last, they had made enough. If the food came out short at that fancy gathering, making the Kings look cheap, Hetty would never let them live the error down.

"One, two, three, four, five," she muttered to herself, "six, seven cherry pies."

Intent upon keeping her count straight, Janet took no notice of her husband walking in through the kitchen door. She'd been working so hard that Alec hadn't the heart to disturb her until now.

"Janet..." he began.

"Two lemon pies...two apple pies..."

"Janet, I need to talk with you."

"Yes, what it is, Alec?" Janet asked distractedly, trying to keep the pies straight in her head and still not looking at him.

"Well...it has to do with Amos Spry."

Janet flung up her hands in annoyance. "Oh...oh dear," she groaned. "Hetty hasn't invited him, too, has she, with his brood?" The Sprys would go through the food like locusts on a rampage! Janet would have to start baking again as fast as she could.

In spite of his troubles, just a flicker of humor touched Alec's mouth.

"No, I don't think she'd invite him."

"That's a relief," Janet sighed, wiping at her forehead with her apron. "She's had me cook enough for half the Island as it is."

"Well, actually," Alec tried again, "it's about the King trust. You see—"

"Trust Hetty to leave all the work to us," Janet flew off again, not even hearing what her husband was trying to say. She walked over to the sink to wash her hands. "Oh, she's just been impossible to deal with since she's taken charge of this ridiculous party."

"I wouldn't worry about the reception, Janet," Alec said, with a wry twist to his lips. There were plenty of bigger things to worry about at the moment. Janet, however, only saw all the work that still had to be done to get the reception set up to Hetty's satisfaction.

"Well, it's all very well for you to tell me not to worry," Janet declared, thinking how obtuse men could be sometimes. "You don't know what it's like to have all these pressures on your mind in my condition. I'm just exhausted, Alec. I've got to go to bed. Could you cover those pies before you come up?"

"Janet, I really need to talk to you."

His message finally penetrated, though not the urgency that went with it. Janet stopped and looked at him with a wide-eyed, exasperated sigh. Alec saw then that she was hot, over-worked and weary from her pregnancy. The last thing she needed was more worries.

"All right," he said, "I can do it." He kissed her lightly on the cheek. "Good night, love."

Janet smiled and hurried upstairs, glad to make her escape from the kitchen.

Alec pulled open a drawer, took out a dish towel, twisted it in his hands a moment, then put it back. He had a better idea. He closed the drawer, reached into the cabinet underneath instead and took out his hidden bottle of whiskey. The King home was a strict Temperance household, and any strong drink found inside it was strictly for medicinal purposes. Alec held the bottle up to the light and decided he was greatly in need of medicinal aid. Tucking the bottle into his back pocket, he picked up his hat and made for the barn.

Sometime later, the gleam of lantern light could be seen through one of the barn windows, and the soft lowing of cattle drifted out on the night air. Alec was in the cow stable, sitting on a milking stool near the shiny new milking machine. He rested his forehead against the warm side of one of the farm's three holstein cows. The level in the whiskey bottle was considerably lower than it had been in the kitchen and Alec looked suspiciously tipsy. The cow lowed and Alec put his finger to his lips in an effort to silence it.

"Shhh! Let's not wake up the whole bloody neighborhood now, huh?" He took a drink from a teacup also purloined from the kitchen. "Here's to ya, girl. I know, I know, I know, it's Roger." He leered over at the milking machine. "Roger and his crazy ideas. He's been my brother for...what is it?...forty years or more, and we still don't get along." He paused and hiccuped, the better to emphasize the point to the cow. "And I've tried. Really, really, I have. I've tried."

The cow, perhaps nervous about getting mixed up in King family squabbles, moved restlessly. When she stepped backward, her heel kicked over the milking machine. It made a satisfying clatter as it fell.

"Right," Alec agreed, taking another swig from the cup. "You don't like it either. Then we won't use it any more."

Chapter Eleven

The next morning, no one had time to notice Alec's hangover—the day of the reception was upon them! All the Kings were swept up into feverish preparations for the guests who would begin arriving that afternoon. Hetty had invited so many people that the reception was to be held outside, on the lawn around the King farmhouse. Mercifully, the weather was fine, making the marquee Hetty had insisted be set up over the tables strictly ornamental.

Janet, who would have preferred to have slept the day away, had been up since dawn rushing about as fast as she could go. Breakfast was no sooner gulped down than the children were pressed into service to get the tables ready. All the best tablecloths—commandeered from the farmhouse and Rose Cottage—were spread over the tables, their ends fluttering softly in the breeze. The children trotted back and forth, bearing pies, cakes, sandwiches, pickles in cut-glass pickle dishes and endless other goodies.

Carrying one of the last loads, Felix made his way anxiously across the lawn balancing a column of china cups and saucers for the tea to be served with dessert. Reaching the table with all items intact, he set the fragile cargo down in relief. Felix was dressed in his best suit, complete with tight bow tie and constricting vest. He tugged at the tie, then noticed the great bowl of whipped cream sitting unguarded, practically next to his elbow. Of course, with all the running about, nobody had bothered to think about lunch, so Felix was starving. It didn't help that he was surrounded by the most tempting dainties the King family could produce. Perpetually hungry, growing boy that he was, he peeped to make sure Olivia's back was turned, licked his fingers and prepared to plunge them into the bowl.

Hetty, zooming in on his blind side, was upon him in a flash.

"Ah! Don't you dare, Felix King!"

Foiled, Felix jumped back guiltily and sped off for another load of cups. Felicity passed him, balancing a cherry pie in each of her hands. She slid the pies onto the table next to where her Aunt Hetty was standing examining the silver-ware. Eagle-eyed for every detail, Hetty pounced upon a serving spoon.

"Felicity, this is dirty," she complained, holding it up to the light, then thrusting it into her niece's hand. "Must be able to see one's face in it, remember? Run inside—get a clean one!"

Felicity, who had been working hard since sunup, looked as though she might have exploded on the spot had her Uncle Roger not appeared just then to view the layout. The spread tables and heaps of food exceeded even his expectations of Hetty's extravagance. His eyes lit up in admiration.

"You've done a remarkable job, Hetty," he said appreciatively. "I am indebted for the warm hospitality."

Hetty flushed happily at praise from her favorite brother. "Really, Roger, it's nothing," she cooed, as though all the bounty around them had simply been conjured from thin air.

Gripping the spoon in her fist, Felicity marched over to where her mother and Felix were now arranging the cups and saucers into rows.

"It's nothing to her, all right," Felicity muttered through gritted teeth, looking back to where Hetty was gushing over Roger. "We do all the work and she gets all the glory."

"Felicity," Janet admonished, but only half-heartedly. Janet was of exactly the same opinion herself and feeling more harried by the minute.

Almost before they knew it, the guests began pouring in, including the reporter and photographer Hetty had made sure to invite from

Halifax. The photographer wasted no time in setting up, and soon Roger was posing stiffly on the lawn.

"Smile, please," the photographer instructed from under the dark cloth that kept light from interfering with the photographic process.

The flash went off. Andrew, Olivia, Sara, Janet and Hetty applauded excitedly, delighted, in spite of everything, to have a celebrity in the family.

"Now," said the reporter, scribbling in his notebook, "maybe we could have one in front of the house where you were born."

The reporter led Roger over to a position in front of the house—and, of course, all the rest of the family followed. Sara and Andrew looked on curiously while Hetty stood beside the children, peacock-like in her moment of glory. Alec, suffering from a headache and the disapproval of his siblings, stood a little further off to view the scene.

"How about one with a close member of the family?" the reporter asked, determined to cover every possible angle for his story.

At this request, Andrew's eyes gleamed with sudden, perfectly natural anticipation. Imagine! Himself and his famous father in the pages of the Halifax *Herald*! That would be proof his father noticed him all right.

As Roger turned to his waiting family, Andrew was already stepping forward, but it wasn't the boy Roger's gaze alighted upon, it was Hetty.

"Come on over here, Hetty," he called out, even as he turned to explain to the reporter, "My sister was the one who pushed me to become a geologist."

Making a feeble attempt at modesty, Hetty hurried over to stand beside her brother.

"Oh, now, Roger's exaggerating," Hetty gushed. "Oh, I'm hardly prepared for this sort of thing," she professed, even though she was wearing her very best dress and had spent a good hour that morning fixing herself up for the occasion. "What must I look like?!"

Hetty beamed into the camera lens, her arm around her favorite brother. Neither of them noticed the dejected look that swept Andrew's face. Olivia noticed, though, and put her hand on Andrew's shoulder in an effort to comfort him.

"It's only a photograph," she whispered.

To Andrew, it was obviously much more, for it meant that Hetty was more important to his father than he was. Alec observed the scene with a sad look, too, but he was hardly in a position to comment about it to either Roger or Hetty.

"Everyone's going to think this was my idea," Hetty chirped.

"Smile, please," the photographer instructed again just before he set off the flash.

Hetty, despite her supposed unpreparedness, turned on a smile like a stage professional. At the same time, nursing his hurt, Andrew turned and walked rapidly away. Anxiously, Olivia watched him leave.

"And again, please," called out the photographer, causing Roger and Hetty to go through their performance yet again, neither of them paying the slightest attention to Andrew.

Standing beside Olivia, Sara, too, watched Andrew go into the barn. When she frowned in concern, Olivia nudged her in his direction.

"Go on," Olivia urged in a whisper. She couldn't very well leave the scene herself, but Sara might be able to cheer the boy up.

Andrew found his way into the barn and slammed the door behind him. In the cow stable, he searched out an empty stall, slipped into it and sank down on the straw, not caring in the least about the effects on his best suit. When the stall door swung shut, he had completely disappeared from sight.

Back at the reception, guests were still arriving. Andrew slipped even further from his father's mind, for Roger and Hetty had no sooner left the photographer than they found themselves buttonholed by two distinguished-looking gentlemen. One was a Professor McKearney, who was looking very interested in Roger, indeed.

"We were just trying to twist Roger's arm into accepting a position at Dalhousie University," he was telling Hetty as he accepted a cup of tea.

Hetty, visibly impressed, managed to swell up another inch or two with pride. How grand to have a university wanting Roger as a member of their faculty!

"Dalhousie? Oh! Afraid you'll be wasting your time, however," she fluttered. "Roger still has significant commitments in Brazil, you see. Don't you, dear?" she asked him importantly.

The professor looked disappointed. He'd hoped that Roger would not be in such strong demand.

"Just for another year," Roger explained, as

though spending time in all sorts of exotic, foreign places was just a part of everyday life for him.

Meanwhile, Sara had made her way to the barn in pursuit of Andrew and was looking through the stalls. At the far end of the stable one of the cows, the very one who had been privy to Alec's drinking bout of the night before, was now lowing continually in a distressed tone. Sara, however, had no time to investigate.

"Andrew?" she called out.

"Just leave me alone!" Andrew muttered from somewhere inside.

Sara went straight to the stall where Andrew was hiding and peered over the top of the door. Andrew was leaning disconsolately against the back wall in the straw, hugging his knees to himself.

"Come on, Andrew," Sara cajoled. "You're missing all of your father's party."

"Who cares?"

These were hardly the words of a boy who rejoiced in his father's success. Sara looked at Andrew more closely.

"Are you all right?"

"He's going away," Andrew muttered, finally getting to the heart of the matter.

"I'm sure it won't be forever," Sara said comfortingly. "Uncle Alec says he'll be back within the year."

Andrew was unimpressed with Sara's attempt to find the bright side.

"That's what he says now, till something more important comes along. I don't know—he just keeps running and running. Maybe things would be different if my mother were still alive."

The cow suddenly let out a bellow that seemed to shake the rafters of the barn. Sara sped out of the stall to look.

"What's the matter with Molly?"

As if to answer, the cow gave a mournful bellow as she crashed about in her stall. Alarmed, Sara bolted from the barn and ran at top speed towards her Uncle Alec, who was talking to Janet on the edge of the crowd.

"Uncle Alec, there's something wrong with one of the cows. She's making an awful noise."

A sick cow was a serious matter to the farm's economy, especially a farm that had only three cows in its herd and had lent all its money to Amos Spry. Alec set off at once with Sara towards the barn.

By now, the other two cows were setting up a ruckus in sympathy with their distressed comrade. As Alec approached Molly, she tossed her head and bawled again, as if to blare that it was about time some help appeared.

"Easy, there, girl. Easy." Alec's voice was soothing as he walked quietly up and rubbed the animal's head. When Molly accepted him, he patted her broad sides and bent down to examine her udder.

Andrew, now worried and curious, too, forgot his own problems long enough to stand up and lean over the door of the stall where he had taken refuge.

"What's wrong with her?" Sara wanted to know.

"Whoa, easy," Alec was saying to the cow as it sidled away from his exploring hand. "I'd say she's got mastitis."

"What's that?" Sara had never heard the dangerous-sounding word before.

"It's an infection of the udder that cows get when they're not milked regularly," Alec told her. "Andrew, when did you last milk this cow?"

Luckily, Andrew had done all his chores and felt he had nothing to hide.

"I used the machine this morning."

"The machine?" Alec scowled suddenly. "Good Lord. Sara, you'd better get me some hot water."

Then Alec turned to Andrew crossly, for he had expressly forbidden the use of the machine in his barn.

"And you had better learn to follow instructions, young man."

As he dashed out the barn door, Andrew looked most upset. He had only tried to be loyal to his father's ideas in using the labor-saving device. What was the point of buying an expensive milking machine if Uncle Alec still wanted all the cows milked by hand?

Chapter Twelve

Troubles, as the proverb says, tend to travel in packs. Hetty was enjoying the reception to the fullest, ushering Roger around, sipping tea with dignitaries and basking in reflected glory, when two men arrived. They certainly weren't invited guests and they certainly weren't in the business of admiring Roger King. In fact, they were the local bailiff and his deputy, making their way purposefully towards Hetty.

"Excuse me," boomed the bailiff, shouldering his way into the middle of a constellation of guests. "Miss Hetty King, is it?"

Hetty, aglow with the triumphs of the day,

turned grandly. She was sipping from one of
Grandmother King's fine bone china cups and
had just been regaling the cream of Avonlea soci-
ety with Roger's accomplishments in Brazil. She
did not take kindly to being interrupted by unin-
vited strangers.

"Yes, I most certainly am," she informed
them in an intimidating tone.

The bailiff, a tall, lugubrious-looking man in
an equally lugubrious black suit, gave a ghost of
a nod. In his profession, he certainly didn't
expect any welcomes.

"Sorry to barge in on you like this, Miss King,
but this is rather urgent official business."

On the bailiff's signal, the deputy whipped
out a grimly official-looking sheet of paper and
handed it to Hetty. Very much annoyed, Hetty
turned back to her guests.

"Would you excuse me a moment?"

Pointing away from the crowd, Hetty gestured to the intruders.

"Why don't we step over here?"

She walked the two men around the screen of
some lilac bushes to get a little privacy and faced
the pair brusquely.

"My good man, what do you mean by coming
in here?" she snapped. "This is private property."

"Apparently," drawled the bailiff, ignoring her temper, "you purchased a milking machine from MacCrae Brothers Agricultural Equipment."

"Yes, I did." And what of it? her look demanded.

"It seems your check was returned, ma'am. There were insufficient funds in your account in Carmody. I'm here to repossess the milking machine."

Hetty's eyes almost popped out from shock. She cast a furtive look at all the assembled guests, most of them local people who would love nothing better than to take home such a scandalous tidbit about the Kings.

"Surely it can all wait for a more—appropriate day," she stuttered, almost whispering now in an attempt to keep the situation from reaching the ears of her company.

The bailiff shook his head. Money matters, as Amos Spry had already found out, never wait for a more appropriate day.

"I'm sorry, ma'am. My instructions are to take the machine away with me, unless you can pay for it...in cash."

Cash! Hetty thought of all the money she had just spent on the reception, and of the very few dollars left in her purse. Embarrassed, and completely flustered, she had no choice but to set out, followed closely by the two men, for the barn.

On the other side of the farmhouse, Felix had finally escaped the social crush and was sitting in peace and quiet under a maple. Not only that, he had finally got his hands on the whipped cream, which was now heaped into an enormous peak smothering the cupcake he clutched in his hand. This reception, Felix decided, might have its benefits after all.

Settling himself luxuriously back against the tree trunk, Felix took an enormous bite out of the cupcake, smearing whipped cream from his nose to his chin. Before he even had a chance to swallow it, though, he caught a glimpse of Andrew tramping out of the house with the fishing basket in his hand. Immediately, Felix heaved himself to his knees.

"Hey!" he shouted. "Where are you going with my fishing basket?"

"None of your business, Felix," Andrew growled back, speeding up his pace.

Andrew's face was knotted with some fearful resolution that did not bode well for the fishing basket. Sara, who had been walking rapidly towards the barn, turned in surprise and started running after Andrew, worried by her cousin's expression. Not to be left out, Felix gulped down the cupcake and sprang to his feet. Whatever concerned the fishing basket also concerned him. He set off after Andrew as fast as his legs could carry him.

The two children caught up with Andrew on the old bridge over the river that ran past the King farm. Andrew, standing by the rail, had opened the basket. Grimly, piece by piece, he was flinging his precious rock collection into the water below.

"Andrew, what are you doing?" Sara panted, remembering what pains Andrew had gone to to put the collection together.

"Dumb rocks!" was all Andrew had to say as he pitched the last bit of quartz furiously into the river.

The splash had barely settled when Andrew swung the fishing basket itself up into the air, clearly intent on slinging it into the river too.

Felix's face contorted with shock. "That's my basket!" he croaked, making a wild dive to save it from a watery fate. He managed to grip one corner and fling himself into a fierce tug-of-war with his cousin.

"It's *my* basket." Andrew shouted, jerking it as hard as he could. "I'll do what I please with it!"

"Andrew!" Sara pleaded, but her voice was unheard over the shuffling and grunting of the two boys.

Andrew, being bigger and older than Felix, and having a far better grip, at last wrenched the basket from Felix's hands and heaved it as far as he could over the rail. Over and over it tumbled in the air before splashing into the murky water below. Felix started turning purple with sheer rage.

"What did you do that for? You stuck-up little Hetty's pet!"

Vengefully, Felix flew at Andrew, trying to grab a great handful of his cousin's hair. Taken by surprise Andrew lost his footing as he tried to fend off his attacker. As he fell, Andrew took Felix with him. The next moment the two boys were rolling about on the bridge pummeling each other for all they were worth. Sara jumped out of range barely in time to avoid being knocked down herself. Seeing how quickly the fight was escalating, she began to wring her hands in distress.

"Felix! Andrew!" she cried frantically. "Someone's gonna get hurt!"

Hurting someone was just what both boys were bent on. Felix was furious about the fishing basket, and Andrew needed to vent all his pent-up frustration about his father's departure. Seeing that she could do nothing herself, Sara turned around and dashed away to get help.

The help she had in mind was her Uncle Alec, who happened, at that moment, to be walking out of the barn. He had changed into his overalls and was so absorbed in his own worries that he all but fell over the bailiff and his deputy, who were coming in pursuit of the milking machine. The bailiff and the deputy were trailed by Hetty and, of course, Roger, who had realized that something was afoot. Hetty was in a state of rage and mortification far too colorful to be described.

"Alec King," she sputtered when she caught sight of her brother, "I have never been so humiliated in all my—Of all things, the bailiff's arrived, in the middle of Roger's reception, to repossess the milking machine!"

If she thought this news was going to jolt Alec, she was in for a surprise. Alec barely looked up.

"Well..." he muttered, thoroughly disgusted with the milking machine and its effects, "let him have it."

Incredibly, Alec started walking on again. Roger stopped him by grabbing his arm.

"Don't give yourself airs, Alec King. This is your fault, and you act like nothing's happened."

Alec was getting very tired of Roger and Hetty's dramatics. He jerked his arm free and nodded back towards the stable.

"Look, we've got a cow in there that might die if I don't get the vet."

"A cow?" croaked Hetty, as though she had never heard of the beasts before.

"Your milking machine—"

Alec choked off the rest of his furious retort before he could say something he'd truly regret. Before he could get anything else out, Sara came barreling along the barnyard fence, shouted urgently through the gate.

"Uncle Alec, Uncle Alec! Andrew and Felix won't stop fighting. Andrew tried to throw Felix into the river!"

Chapter Thirteen

Wondering what new plagues could fall upon them next, Hetty, Roger and Alec sped off behind Sara towards the bridge to deal with this latest crisis. Sara's urgency had left them in no doubt that this was a matter that must be taken in hand.

"Sara!" Hetty called out in a vain attempt to make the fleet little girl wait for her.

Alec was the first of the party to reach the scene of the struggle. Felix and Andrew were still down on the planks, writhing in the dust and yanking ferociously at each other's good clothes. Alec glowered down at the twisting bodies.

"All right, boys, stop that," he ordered curtly. "Stop that right now, both of you. Come on."

The two boys were so wrought up they didn't even hear Alec. When his words had no effect, Alec grabbed Felix by the collar and forcibly lifted him away from his cousin. Luckily for Felix, Roger arrived in time to do the same to Andrew. The two men managed to pull their sons apart and set them upright on their feet a safe distance away from each other. Both boys were breathing hotly, and Felix sported a bloody nose.

"Felix, you know better than to get into fights," Alec chided severely.

Felix was not about to be done out of his grievance—not even when suspended from his father's fist. He lashed out an accusing finger at Andrew.

"He tossed his stupid rock collection in the river, and Grandpa King's fishing basket too. Look!" He pointed over the bridge to where the basket bobbed and rocked in the current, growing more waterlogged by the minute.

Hetty's hands flew to her mouth for, despite its decrepit state, the basket really was one of the King family treasures. "Andrew!" she gasped.

Roger gave his son a shake. "What'd you do that for, Andrew?"

Andrew only fixed his mouth stubbornly and refused to reply. Alec, quite at the end of his rope, answered for him.

"Because he can't stand the blasted rock collection," he shouted at his brother. "Until a few weeks ago, he had no interest in rocks at all. He's just trying to please you."

Roger let go of Andrew and straightened up, startled by such a farfetched idea. Like a lot of fathers, he tended to think of his son as an exact replica of himself, and he hadn't exactly taken the time to discover otherwise.

"That's ridiculous. He's always loved geology. It's your fault, you damn fool. Since he's been in Avonlea, you've done nothing but turn him against me."

Alec released Felix's collar so abruptly that Felix staggered to keep his footing. Like Felix, Alec had a lot of pressures built up inside of him, and it was only natural that he, too, should reach his limit. At this wild accusation from Roger, Alec stepped forward furiously.

"Well, if you really believe that, why are you letting him stay here with me now? Answer me that, Mr. Internationally Renowned Geologist."

"Alec, stop that!" Hetty hissed, embarrassed at such dissension among the adults of the family.

In turn, Roger grew even angrier than Alec. Anger was a splendid way to keep from really thinking about whether or not there was any truth in Alec's words.

"You make me sick!" Roger spat out, going on the attack. "Now I realize the mistake I've made leaving Andrew with someone who can't even look after himself, let alone his family."

Never had the contrast between the two brothers been more vivid—Alec in his well-worn farm overalls, Roger with his fine suit and educated sophistication. Alec had had his fill of Roger's airs of superiority. He jabbed his finger fiercely towards Roger's game leg, ready to drop a few home truths on his pampered brother.

"Just because of that blasted accident, you've taken your frustrations out on me. Well, I've had enough! You've got a chip on your shoulder that gets bigger and uglier the older you get."

"Alec! Roger!" Hetty admonished rather desperately. "You're both behaving like a couple of children."

"Father would roll over in his grave if he ever knew what a failure you are," Roger shot recklessly back at Alec.

The two men stood head to head, exactly as Felix and Andrew had done moments earlier. Alec gave Roger a shove, perhaps remembering, like Felix, all the extra work he had been stuck with as a boy because Roger had been above such menial tasks and busy with his books.

"You're so full of yourself, you can't see past your nose. You wouldn't lift a shovel with that bum leg of yours."

"You weren't the one dropped when you were a child," Roger retorted, as if that made up for all the special treatment and privileges he had received.

"Well, sometimes," Alec shouted, "I wish I

was, because then I wouldn't have to listen to you complaining about it forever."

Roger's face and neck turned scarlet. Fury made him breathe very hard. He seemed to have no arguments left except physical ones.

"Well, maybe you ought to know what it's like!"

Without warning, Roger grabbed Alec by the shoulders and pushed him sideways, over to the side of the bridge against the railing. The railing was old and certainly not designed to take the weight of two belligerent men. In protest, it promptly sagged, cracked and broke away. For a moment, the two men seemed to hang, suspended in the air, astonishment stamped upon their faces. Then Alec's body tore from Roger's grip and went spinning down into the water below.

A dunking in the warm, shallow river might have been harmless enough had Alec not plummeted straight to the bottom and struck his head on a rock. When he surfaced, he lay motionless in the water, face down in the churning backwash his fall had caused. The rest of the family stood frozen on the bridge, gaping down through the splintered railing, unable to believe what had just happened.

Andrew was the first one to come to life. He sprang forward. "Uncle Alec?" he called, fully expecting his uncle to shake himself upright, find a footing on the rocky riverbed and come sloshing out onto the grassy bank at the side.

But Alec remained unmoving; only the agitation of the water caused him to bob up and down. His arms hung limp and his hair haloed his head like seaweed. Each fraction of a second that passed seemed to stretch into an age.

It was Hetty who first realized that Alec was unconscious. She began to jerk frantically at Roger's sleeve.

"Roger! Roger, do something!"

"He's drowning!" Felix shrieked, suddenly turning pale and forgetting everything else but his father's danger. "He's drowning!"

"Roger!" Hetty pleaded, staring down in horror at the limp body floating below.

Roger had been turning pale himself in a panic at what he had just done. Hetty's prods at last galvanized him into action. Freed from his paralysis, he rushed round the end of the bridge and down the steep riverbank towards the water, losing his hat and tearing off his jacket as he went. In spite of his game leg, he moved with amazing quickness, half hopping, half sliding over the ledges of rock and crumbling earth until he, too, crashed into the water. Without a thought for his elegant white suit, Roger waded in, grabbed Alec by the shoulders and dragged him backward towards the shore.

By this time, all the others had scrambled down the bank too, getting smeared all over with grass stains and muddy earth. A row of willing hands were extended to help haul Alec's heavy and awkward weight out of the water. But when they did, Alec only sagged slackly onto the grass, as unmoving as he had been in the water. Rivulets poured from his hair and his clothes. A great gash on his temple glared in the streaming expanse of his face.

For a moment, it looked as though panic were going to paralyze everyone again while Alec suffocated on the water in his lungs before their very eyes. However, Hetty had not been a schoolteacher for years, teaching the rules of water safety, for nothing. Fast action was needed by someone who knew what she was doing. Pushing the others aside, Hetty took command.

"Lay him over this boulder, Roger," she ordered, already rolling up her sleeves. "Face down."

As he had done so often before, Roger hurried to obey his older sister. He heaved Alec up over a large rock so that his head was hanging down on the other side. Hetty, veteran of a thousand schoolyard emergencies, grabbed Alec around the waist to pump water out of his lungs.

"One, two, three..." she panted, straining against her brother's ribcage with all her strength.

Felix was shaking, Sara was white as a handkerchief, and Andrew was unable to move. Everyone watched in horrible apprehension while Hetty struggled with Alec's bulk. Time stood still as Hetty pumped, and still Alec didn't move.

Then, just when Felix was about to burst into howls, Alec twitched, sputtered and began to cough. Immense relief swept over the group. The children broke into enormous smiles. Roger released the breath that had been strangling in his own chest, and Hetty burst into tears.

Alec, the farmer, had turned out to be just as precious to Hetty as Roger, the famous geologist. She realized she had been behaving like a fool in the last few days, siding with one against the other. She was done, once and for all, with playing favorites.

Chapter Fourteen

Later in the evening, after the reception had broken up and the milking machine had been hauled off in the back of the bailiff's buggy, Alec managed to escape to the barn to tend the sick cow. In all the to-do over bandaging Alec's head and poking and prodding to make sure he was really all right, no one had cared very much what the bailiff took, and the vet had been and gone, leaving Molly feeling that humans might have their good points after all. Now, hoping to get a little peace and quiet himself, Alec sat down on the stool beside the cow, holding up the lantern and stroking her soft side.

As Alec sat in contemplation, the white bandage glimmering on his head, footsteps sounded behind him. It was Roger, holding another lantern and looking troubled. He stood a long moment, looking at his brother, before clearing his throat. At the sound, Alec glanced over.

"How's the patient?" Roger inquired by way of breaking the ice.

The previous jagged tension between the two men seemed to have changed, replaced now by a mixture of careful civility and great awkwardness. Dressed in his old clothes, Roger no longer seemed the celebrated geologist, but more like a contrite younger brother who had got himself into trouble and was now wondering how to put things right.

"Oh, I think she'll be fine. Doc Griffith's got the swelling down and, uh..."

"I...wasn't referring to the cow," Roger broke in, shifting uneasily on his feet again.

"Me?" Alec exclaimed. "I'm as solid as a rock, Roger. You know all about rocks, don't you?"

"Obviously not enough, Alec," Roger replied diffidently. "You know, for a second there I...I thought I..." He swallowed, pausing emotionally. "You were nearly killed."

"But then, thanks to you, I wasn't," Alec returned slowly.

The moment he had returned to consciousness, everyone had rushed to tell him how Roger had been the one to pull him from the water.

Roger put down the lantern as though he were having trouble holding it steady. He had had quite a bit of time to think about what had nearly happened at the river, and he'd grown shakier about it with each passing hour.

"It would've been my fault." He ran his fingers distractedly through his hair. "I just don't know what came over me. I..." He stumbled again, then asked simply, "Can you ever forgive me?"

Out of the corner of his eye, Alec spotted Andrew as he came into the barn and start pitching hay into a manger. He thought of all the sad consequences when members of a family don't make up with each other. Slowly, he put down his lantern and rose to his feet.

"You're my brother," Alec said with a tremble in his voice. "You always will be."

Alec put his arms around Roger and hugged him. Brothers and sisters were precious, no matter how annoying they might become at times. Roger looked Alec straight in the eye, then looked over at Andrew, as though he had just come to the same conclusion about sons.

Seeing the direction of Roger's thoughts, Alec smiled, gave Molly a final pat and made his way back to the house, to leave Andrew alone with his father. Roger walked over to the hay pile, grabbed another pitchfork and started helping his son.

"I always hated this job when I was your age," he said to Andrew, trying to make conversation—something he hadn't had a lot of practice at with the boy.

"It isn't very important, is it?" Andrew said, plunging his fork deep into the loose hay. Certainly not as important as the work of a famous geologist, he thought.

Roger smiled ruefully. "It is to the cows."

For all his inner turmoil, Andrew couldn't help grinning at this. Encouraged, Roger spoke again.

"Andrew, I've been thinking about my going back to Brazil."

Andrew's face closed up again, though he strove to be brave. His father was going to leave him again, and there didn't seem to be a thing he could do about it.

"I understand why you have to go back. I'll just miss you, that's all."

Roger shook his head. He had done more thinking that afternoon, it seemed, than he had since Andrew's mother had died.

"I am not going to allow you to miss me any more, son," he declared, tossing a huge forkful of hay.

Seeing the surprise and sudden, shining hope in Andrew's face, Roger wondered how he could have been so blind for so long to the boy's needs.

Once the process of forgiveness got started, it couldn't stop until the whole family was included. The next day, all tidied up for dinner, Felix wandered into the sun room, where he whiled away the time by lining up his tin soldiers atop the little mahogany table. He knocked over a couple of battalion leaders, though, when Andrew walked in carrying, of all things, Grandpa King's fishing basket. Andrew set the basket down on the table beside Felix.

"Where'd you get that?" Felix inquired, trying to decide whether or not he should start getting angry again.

"Took a while, but I found it downstream in the reeds. I want to show you something."

Felix went pointedly back to his soldiers, supposing that Andrew had just started another collection of something or other to impress his father. And Felix sure wasn't going to give Andrew the satisfaction of looking into a basket that he still stubbornly thought of as rightfully his own.

"No, thanks. I've seen enough of your dumb rocks."

"Come on, Felix. Open it."

Remembering his scuffle with Andrew, Felix wasn't sure he should have any part of this. Both boys had been subdued since the incident on the bridge and had studiously avoided each other.

Now, though, Andrew was insisting that Felix look inside the basket. Curiosity fought with reluctance and finally won.

"All right," Felix grumbled, reaching for the lid.

The basket looked little the worse for its watery adventure, and inside, it certainly held a surprise. The interior was full of new fishing lines, a float, flies, hooks and just about everything a boy would need for a happy afternoon on the riverbank. Felix's eyes widened.

"What's this?" he cried in astonishment.

Andrew grinned, delighted with the effect of the fishing gear. "Maybe you can take me fishing tomorrow and we can both use it."

It took only a second for Felix to digest the full meaning of Andrew's offer.

"Yeah," he agreed, pleased with the idea that they might share the basket. He wasn't a greedy boy. It had been the principle of the thing that had got him so riled up. And, oh, it felt so very good to be friends with his cousin once again!

The call to dinner interrupted further examination of the basket's contents. Both boys, hungry as usual, dashed into the kitchen, where the rest of the family had seated themselves around the big kitchen table. Hetty, in the interests of health, spooned cauliflower onto Felix's plate, completely ignoring his grimaces.

"Sara," she said, turning towards her with the cauliflower spoon.

"Make sure you eat those vegetables, now," Alec said to Felicity, winking.

"Sara, cauliflower—your favorite," Hetty said, beginning to load the white vegetable onto Sara's plate. Hetty had lots of ironclad opinions about what children should eat.

"Thank you," Sara murmured, having no other choice.

Andrew had squeezed himself in beside his father. Now the two sat close, heads together, apparently conspiring happily about something.

"Are you sure about this, now?" Roger whispered, fending off the cauliflower bowl.

"Yes, Papa," Andrew whispered back, nodding.

"All right." Roger cleared his throat and tapped his glass with his spoon to get everyone's attention. "Please, everyone, there's something I'd like to say."

Looking fondly at Andrew beside him, he placed a hand on the boy's shoulder.

"Andrew and I have discussed something. We've decided I should accept the position offered me at Dalhousie University next fall."

Olivia, Hetty, Alec and all the children responded with delight. They really didn't like a member of their family away in Brazil any more than Andrew did.

"Oh, Roger!" laughed Olivia, clasping her hands together.

"Oh!" Hetty was so overwhelmed that she had to press a hand to her bosom to contain her joy. It would be wonderful to have Roger so nearby. And a member of a university faculty, too! That would certainly enhance the family's prestige!

"I would like," Roger announced, holding up his hand, "to thank all of you for the generosity..." he smiled at Janet, "...the friendship..." he said, turning to Hetty, and then looking at Alec "...and the leadership you've extended to Andrew over the past year." Roger smiled warmly at his brother. "We all owe Alec a great deal. Please, raise your glasses in a toast to Alec!"

Just as all the glasses were halfway into the air and Alec beaming so broadly his face was fit to split, a clatter of steps was heard at the kitchen door.

"Alec! Alec!" an eager voice called out, and Amos Spry walked in, with young Stephen at his heels.

"Oh..." Amos faltered, coming to a dubious

halt before the family scene. "I'm sorry. I didn't think you'd be having dinner yet. This'll wait."

He was about to hustle Stephen straight outside again when Alec beckoned expansively. Alec wouldn't hear of a neighbor leaving the King house like that.

"Amos, come on in here."

Amos paused at the door and turned back uncertainly, removing his own battered cap and the one Stephen wore. Then, straightening a little, he reached into his own pocket and handed Alec an envelope. A certain pride was stamped on Amos's face.

"It's not all of it, but it's as much as I could get by without."

Alec took the envelope slowly. He hadn't expected to see any hard cash for weeks yet.

"You didn't have to pay it back right away," Alec said, knowing how much Amos must have scrambled to gather the money.

Amos ducked his head, keeping a wary eye on Hetty. He knew very well what Hetty must have thought about the loan.

"Well, thanks to your help, over the past couple of weeks I've made more than enough from just half my crop. I'll give you the rest at the end of the season."

Alec could have been forgiven for a triumphant glance at his family, but he refrained. He was only happy that Amos Spry had found some luck at last.

"That's good news, Amos. Thank you."

Wonder of wonders, Hetty and Roger smiled at each other and Roger got up from the table to fetch two more glasses.

"No, no, no. It's you I gotta thank," Amos protested. "There's few in Avonlea who'd do what you done, Alec."

Sara Stanley had eyes only for the envelope in Alec's hand. "Oh, good, Aunt Hetty," she crowed. "Now we can get that milking machine back."

Hetty's hand flew up as if she were trying to wave the very idea away. Nervously, she glanced at Alec.

"Oh, well," she mumbled, "I...I think we'll let your Uncle Alec decide that, Sara."

Having thus been reinstated as chief of farming operations, Alec grinned at Hetty while Roger handed two glasses of cordial to Amos and Stephen.

"Perhaps you'd like to join us in a toast," he said to them.

"Oh...uh..."

"Raise your glasses," Roger called out, lifting his own.

Amos was not exactly at home with toasts. He gulped hard, then managed to lift his glass, too.

"To Alec King," Amos said, with a hearty sincerity felt all around the room. There could be no doubt that, in Amos's mind, anyway, Alec King was one of the most special people on the whole Island.

Everyone, even Hetty, raised their glasses, too. And they all agreed with Amos's opinion.

Alec looked at his neighbor and shook his head. "To Amos Spry," he boomed, returning the compliment. All glasses were raised again.

"To your health," Amos said, trying to keep the cordial from sloshing over the rim of the glass.

"Good health," echoed Alec.

Everyone drank the toast heartily, only too glad to have real family harmony restored.

Harmony had its practical results, as well. Felix and Andrew exchanged a glance as they hurried through their meal. They wolfed down dessert too—apple pie left over from the reception. The minute they could be excused, they rushed off to the river, fishing poles in hand, the precious basket carried between them.

Felix found his favorite spot on the bank and prepared to introduce Andrew to the fine art of fishing—something he felt every King ought to know. As the basket stood open, revealing its treasures, it was almost as though Grandpa King himself were standing there, passing on a bit of wisdom that all boys, whether young or all grown up, had to learn. Andrew and Felix were certainly wiser now, even if at the expense of nearly bashing each other senseless on the bridge. How very much more pleasant, they were both thinking as they cast their lines out companionably in the afternoon sun, to share something precious than to sit all alone foolishly trying to keep it to oneself.

🍏　　🍏　　🍏